PICKPOCKET

An AGAINST THE ODDS Novel

CHRISTA DeCLUE

Editor: All About the Edits
Cover Designer: Furious Fotog
Publisher: Epistula Publishing

DEDICATION

To my family, you all are my driving force.
To everyone I love, thank you for believing in me.

ONE

ZAYDRA

I'M GOING TO FREEZE MY NIPPLES OFF.

It's been hovering at around thirty-five degrees the whole morning but now that night has fallen, it's dropped down to "cold as balls" with a side of "fuck this." I pull my threadbare coat tighter and shiver as I gaze down the bustling St. Louis street. There are too many people, but not many marks. It's not easy being a certified "borrower of things," which is the best way to say I'm a pickpocket. People in groups are harder to pick from, someone always notices, but if I pick a loner, it's easier. All I have to do is brush up against them or "accidentally" knock into someone, and they never notice they're lighter by a single item until I'm long gone—in my experience, that is.

As I continue to scan people covertly, the first flakes of snow begin to fall, and at the same time, my stomach decides to growl uncomfortably. I haven't eaten in two days and if I don't find a mark soon, I won't eat tonight either. The cobblestone street, full of people, is slowly clearing as snow starts to dust the ground. I begin walking a tiny bit faster, when I spot him. He is mouthwateringly gorgeous, a couple inches over six feet, with sandy brown hair and cerulean blue eyes—ones that remind me of the emerald coast that used to be my home. He's muscular, with broad shoulders, and I want to climb him, like my favorite oak tree in my childhood front yard.

The two best things about this random stranger? He looks like money—clean-cut and wearing expensive clothes—and he's alone and talking on the phone. Distraction is perfect for a borrower. I make my way closer, keeping my head slightly bent as he stalks towards me, talking heatedly into his phone, low enough I can't make out what he's saying. I see my opportunity and take it, tripping over my own two feet, straight into Mr. Let Me Sit On Your Face, who drops his phone to steady me. He grabs me by my shoulders and my body tingles, but my hands are fast, from his pocket to mine. I have his wallet.

Mission accomplished.

"I'm so sorry, sir. I swear, all this snow makes me clumsier than I already am." I look up at him from beneath my lashes.

"It's fine, ma'am, are you all right? You smacked into me pretty hard." He runs his hand along my arm and I'm momentarily stupefied. His eyes are like lasers, seeing into my soul. I'm positive he's not going to like anything past the surface, though. My demons don't play well with others, they never have.

"I did smash into you, and you are hard. I mean, I'm hard. I mean, you're like smashing into a brick wall. Oh Jesus, I'm going to stop talking now," I stutter. *What is wrong with me?* He stumps me in a way a man never has, and I need to break away fast before he notices his wallet is missing.

"I really need to go. I'm so sorry for knocking in to you." I quickly pick up his phone from the snow-dusted sidewalk and hand it to him. "Here's your phone."

I hurriedly walk away, but I can feel his eyes on me, so I add a little sashay to my step. While I shouldn't want him to remember me, because hello, I just stole from the dude, a small part of me wants him to. I round two corners and pull out the wallet. The first thing I pull out is a folded-up slip of paper. Curiosity gets the better of me and I unfold and read it quickly. Deciding it's unimportant, I toss it and the rest of the wallet into the garbage, after I pull out five crisp one-hundred-dollar bills. I never use credit or debit cards but I do take the money. To men like him, it's chump change.

I hide the wallet underneath other garbage, not wanting anyone else to take advantage of the situation. Hey, I'm a thief with a bit of a conscience, sue me.

My tummy growls, demanding food, so I head down the street in search of something to eat.

TWO

COLLIN

I'M STILL STARING AFTER THE CURVY BRUNETTE WITH THE vivid green eyes when my phone rings in my hand. I fumble to answer. Shit, I can't afford to get distracted by some chick. Not when I have bigger problems.

"Hey, Ryan. I went to this meeting with the guy you tipped me off about, but he gave me a piece of paper that he told me not to open until I was alone. What the fuck, dude? He was twitchy too." I exhale roughly and rub my tired eyes as I turn to walk back down the slowly quieting street.

"I told you, Collin, if anybody knows where Cammie is, it's that guy. He's the only one I know still alive with connections to that trafficking ring. We've tried like hell to get a guy undercover, but they're good and we can't pin their location down. I figured he'd talk to you because you're not a cop or a Fed," Ryan says.

I pass a few people, my mind elsewhere, as I think about my sweet little niece and where the fuck these assholes have taken her. Cammie is only thirteen, and at first, I thought she ran away. She's a good kid, but was upset she didn't know her father, and I figured she was acting out. My twin sister, Collette, didn't think so.

As it turned out, she was right. Cammie was grabbed outside the mall, in this very city, six months ago. And the fuckers sent me a note to gloat about it, because I'm known, because I have fucking money. This is a game to them, and apparently, they think I won't move heaven and earth to get my niece back.

"And grab a coffee, because it's probably going to be a long night after you read that message." Ryan's voice sounds in my ear, bringing me back to the conversation.

"Yeah, okay, dude. Please keep feelers out, in case they surface. Collette needs her back, and I need her safe."

Hanging up, I stop at the corner Starbucks. When I make it to the front of the line, I reach for my wallet and stop cold. I start searching my front and back pockets but come up empty. My wallet is gone. My fucking wallet, with the only lead I've had on Cammie in months, is just *gone*.

I step out of line with an apologetic smile to the barista and try to keep a lid on the fury attempting to boil over. The only way I wouldn't have noticed someone stealing it was if they…*no*. My mind raced to the curvy brunette, who was wearing worn, thin clothes. She was beautiful, with the fullest lips I had ever seen, and that kept me from noticing the hungry beat down look about her. She was curvy but thin, as if she hadn't eaten. As if she had nothing to lose by stealing from a stranger.

"*Fuck!*" I roar as I take off out the door, causing people to jump out of my way.

I run a couple of blocks in the direction I saw her walking. I don't see her, but it couldn't have been more than ten minutes, so she had to be here! My eyes search the empty alleys and passing restaurants. Then I see her walking out of a sandwich shop across the street, down the block a short distance.

I'm about to sprint for her, when I see a police officer in front of me. I figure telling him will cover my bases, in case someone calls the cops about a man chasing a woman through the streets of St. Louis. I jog over to him, and grit out, "That woman over there, that brunette with the green patched jacket, she stole my wallet!"

I guess I'm louder than I thought because as I point to her, she notices me. Her wide, green eyes grow larger and she takes off running. The police officer gives chase, yelling, "Ma'am, *stop!* Police!"

I follow behind at a slightly slower pace, dodging people fumbling to get out of the way. The police officer catches up with her and grabs her by the arm. She breaks his hold easily, as if she's done it before, and when she turns to run, he grabs her by the hair and yanks. I don't know why, but I find I'm holding myself back from hitting him. Even though she stole from me, I don't want anyone hurting her.

It's such a strange dilemma, but I don't have time to contemplate it as she rears back and clocks him in the face with the strength of a caged wild animal rather than a woman who is a few inches over five feet. I hear a *crunch* and see blood spurt, and the officer grabs for his nose as she sprints away. The officer tells me to wait while he radios for backup to find this woman who just assaulted him and made me hard in the process. What can I say, I'm a sick bastard.

After several minutes, a few other officers arrive on the scene and spread out, scouring the streets of downtown St. Louis. I pray they find her, so I can get back the information she stole from me. I don't give a damn about the money, she can have it, but I need to find my niece. Strangely enough, I want to see her beautiful, haunting face again too.

A rookie officer takes down my information and tells me they'll call when they catch her, that I would be better off heading home because if she's homeless, she most likely knows the streets best. Feeling my niece's whereabouts slipping through my fingers, I do as he suggests, a little more desolate than I was an hour ago.

I feel my rage building and at that moment, I could strangle the little thief. But I won't because one, I'm not that type of man, and two, because she has the only known clue to Cammie at this point. I hate I was bewitched enough by her to ignore all the training I ever had in the Special Forces. In normal circumstances, I'm more leery and much more fucking aware of my surroundings. At any given moment, I always know how many people are in the immediate vicinity, and where all the fucking exits are. One pair of green eyes and full lips, and I can't remember my own name. Ryan will laugh me out of his office and then punch me twice—once in the face, and once in the dick.

Fuck, I need a drink.

THREE

ZAYDRA

I'M REALLY REGRETTING STOPPING FOR THAT SANDWICH SO close to the scene of the crime. My lungs burn and my stomach rebels from sprinting for so long. I weave in and out of passersby, and dodge trashcans and small children. The cops aren't currently behind me, but they've seen my face. And I'm pretty sure breaking a cop's nose is frowned upon. My bad, but yanking me back by the hair is one of my triggers, and I can't be held responsible for my actions at that point. Not that I expect my reasoning to hold up in court. I sigh, frustrated, because now I'm going to have to leave this city. I swipe the snowflakes off my face in aggravation.

Fuck a duck. I actually like it here in St. Louis.

There are usually a lot of marks and enough places to squat in. I haven't even been here two months yet, and I can feel my inner pout breaking free at the predicament I've gotten myself into. I'm usually much more careful when borrowing from people, but hunger made me sloppy. What's even worse is, I lost the damn sandwich I bought in the chase.

I lost count of the "Hey, watch it" comments I've gotten as I've been sprinting away, but it's getting harder to run. Not only because my legs are cramping and my energy is waning from hunger, but the sidewalk is getting slippery from the snow and the flakes are getting bigger. I need to stop and hide, so I round a corner and head into an alleyway. I've been here over a month now, so I've gotten to know this city pretty well.

With the last bit of energy I have, I leap up and grab the fire escape ladder. I pull it down and start climbing with my legs shaking and my strength starting to leave me, I finally make it to the third story, and pull up a window. This apartment is vacant so I've stayed here the past few nights. I heft myself up and over the sill into the room awaiting me, with the grace of a newborn calf. I sprawl face first on the floor for a few minutes before I roll over.

My little bundle of items is still in the corner where I left it, next to my threadbare blanket I've been using as a bed. I need to leave in the morning, but tonight, I need sleep, to regain my energy. There is no electricity, so I crawl over to light the small candle I have, and wrap myself in my smaller blanket to try to keep warm. I pull out the only picture I have of my mother from my bundle, and touch the glossy but weathered portion that is her smiling face. I send up a small prayer she's still proud of me, regardless of the things I do. That she still loves me. She's holding me in the picture, like she always would, so I try not to worry. I wipe away one stray tear with the back of my cold, shaking hand, as I put her picture away.

I lie down on the blanket and try to get comfortable, willing myself not to freeze to death as I curl into a ball. I don't how long I lay there before sleep finally begins to pull me under, but it's a while. As I drift off, one image is in my head—the man on the street's face. His ID said his name is Collin Reeves. His gorgeous face was furious, almost frantic, which is most people's reaction to losing a wallet, but to a man like him, it should be nothing more than an annoyance. The frantic look on his face has me feeling more guilt than I have in a long time. My last thought before dreams take me is that if I lived a normal life, I'd let him own me.

The heat and strength of my arousal builds as he kisses me like he's a drowning man. I start to ride his thigh to give myself some relief, and I cry out as my clit finally finds the exact friction it needs. A bolt of lust shoots to my core and I can feel my wetness soaking my pussy and his thigh, as he kisses down to my throat while restraining my body with one hand. The other hand travels down to find my pussy, and he pulls me away from his thigh. I make a disgruntled noise and he laughs hoarsely as he palms me. I can feel the heat of his hand, and I run my own over his broad, muscled back, hoping to seduce him into giving me what I need. I can't reach his cock, or I would have my hands all over him.

He captures my mouth in another searing kiss as he begins to lightly stroke my clit. My body is bound so tightly, I might die if he doesn't stop teasing me. With his tongue against mine, he mimics what I want him to do to my pussy. I struggle to find his cock with my hands. Realizing what I intend, he uses both hands to restrain me, and fuck, if that doesn't make me hotter. He uses his body weight to press me down into the mattress and starts caressing my body with both hands.

When he pinches my nipple with one hand, he brings his mouth down to suck the other, which makes me moan and squirm. I can feel the wetness from my pussy leak to my thighs. As he raises his head, those blue eyes sear into me as he begins to spread me wide with his fingers. I moan loudly and he grins down at me. As soon as I decide to beg him, he slides two fingers deep inside.

It's electrifying to my little pussy and I can feel the pleasure building higher, as he pumps his fingers in and out in a rhythm that I would love for him to use with his cock. Speaking of the monster, I feel him grow harder on my thigh, and I sneak my hand down in between us until I circle him with my fingers.

He's so large it's hard for me to fit my fingers around him, and so long I might just propose to him right there, if he can finally make me come and stop teasing me. He groans deep in his throat as I start to stroke him from root to tip, and he gives me a salacious grin. My mind is fogged by my own lust, enough to where I didn't see his other hand move until he brings it down with a hard smack on my ass. I yelp when I feel the sting so I glare up at him, but if it's even possible, my pussy gets wetter around his fingers and I feel the tightening as if I could come any moment.

He increases the speed of his fingers as he brings his head down to suck my nipple into his mouth. I feel the pulls from his lips deep into my belly, and just as the pleasure tightens to a breaking point, he flicks my clit with his other hand, and I shatter, screaming out, "Collin!"

I jerk upright and scan the room, slightly lit by the glow of my tiny candle. No one is there and the only thing I can hear besides the honking of horns outside is my own erratic, harsh breathing. I no longer feel the cold because of the blood rushing through my body at fast speeds. I'm warm and covered in my own sweat, and my pussy is still seeping wetness into my scrap of panties, making me realize I just got off from a dream of a man I stole from, without any stimulation. A man I hope to never see again. I'm ten kinds of fucked up but my body is still humming from the strength of my orgasm, and I hate that I woke up before I felt him inside of me. I have a traitorous brain, and for damn sure, a traitorous body.

I blow out my little candle, then try to fall back to sleep, the only light in the tiny bedroom from the streetlight outside. My mind is still racing, but I will my body to calm. The sexy-as-fuck look in his eyes from my dream keeps flashing through my mind. I wish my life was different, so I could find him and fuck him. He's the first man I've been interested in as anything other than a mark in a long while.

Too bad I already stole from him, and too bad my life has no looks of changing. Such is life, what can I do. I'll keep dreaming of Mr. Let Me Sit on Your Face, and that will have to be enough. I finally start to succumb to sleep after a long while, and when the adrenaline finally gives out, I can't help but wish I was in that soft bed with that hard man.

FOUR

ZAYDRA

As my mind slowly comes awake and awareness of the day filters into my body, I blink open my eyes, and slowly rise, despite my protesting muscles. I stretch and moan as my back pops. I get to my feet and go to pee, before I start my long day of leaving. As soon as I finish—thankfully, they left the water on in this apartment—I do some stretches and exercises to keep my body limber and the methodical movements ease my brain of most of the worry of getting caught. I'm still slightly lethargic from the cold and lack of energy, so I return to the window and look outside. The amount of snow on the ground, and the sheer vastness of the white puffy mounds has me groaning. Motherfucker, leaving today is going to be a challenge. I put my second jacket on over my first, then change into my goodwill combat boots and head out.

Trudging through snow in Missouri is a heinous bitch. It's cold and wet, and I hate every aspect of it besides the beauty. I make it to a small bakery, a couple blocks from downtown, and order a coffee and a muffin, but keep my hood up in case any of the boys in blue decide to show up. I shuck the cold sitting at the little booth, and as I look around, I lock eyes with a younger man, so I sweetly ask to borrow his phone to map the quickest way to the bus station.

As soon as I know where I'm going, I give the phone back to the poor sap, who is now looking at me like I'm a meal. He starts to ask for my number and I politely shake my head, gathering my things then turning to leave. Some guys just aren't very bright—if I'm borrowing his phone, how would I have a number? I make it just outside the door and into the frigid wind, when I hear, "*Freeze!*"

It startles me enough, I drop my muffin and my coffee. Dirty fuckballs!

I would have laughed from the irony of telling me to freeze, as snow is falling around me, but I'm faced with the sight of an irate policeman who has two black eyes and a swollen nose. Oh, and a drawn gun. To quote my favorite commercial, son of a biscuit-eating bulldog. I'm in trouble and I'm really not in a position to run in ankle-deep snow. I raise my hands in the classic, "don't shoot" move and heave a giant sigh. "Come cuff me, honey. We both know I can't run in snow like this without falling."

He cautiously makes his way over to me, as if I'm going to pop up and ninja his ass. To be honest, I probably could, but I have no chance of making it to the bus station before Sparky here, or one of his buddies, gets to me. I really want to though, as I look longingly at the dropped muffin on the ground. When he reaches me, he holsters his gun and breaks out the metal handcuffs. As I feel the cold steel snap into place, my snarkiness gets the better of me.

"Kinky. Why, Officer, at least buy me dinner before we get into fetishes." For that, Officer Sparky pushes my face into the freezing cold and wet snow. I guess I need to work on my comedic timing. Who knew?

I decide not to tell him my safe word because at this point, he doesn't seem to care. I mean, how rude. I can't be the first person to give him a black eye. *He just has one of those faces*, I think to myself. The punchable ones that make you irrationally upset. It's long, with beady eyes—when they're not black with bruises, that is.

He trudges me over to the police car around the corner. His partner scrambles out of the car, takes one look at his partner's face, and opens the door to the back seat. "Such a nice man to open the door for a lady. You could teach Officer Sparky here some manners, I'm sure," I tell him innocently.

Officer Sparks grunts and all but tosses me into the back of the police car. The door slams with a *thud* and these cuffs are on tight. And of course, now I have to pee again. What...the French...toast.

FIVE

COLLIN

I GROAN AS I SLOWLY COME AWAKE, GREETED BY A pounding head and my living room floor. The carpet against my cheek is soft enough, but it's still not comfortable enough for a prolonged stay. My head feels like it's going to explode and I have the worst cotton mouth in history. I take inventory of the two bottles of bourbon surrounding me, and groan again, then bring my head to my hands as I sit up and close my eyes. My dinner from last night threatens to come back up, but thankfully, most of the spinning has stopped, though my brain feels like it's in a fish bowl. I'm too old to be drinking until I pass out but with the night I had, I can't bring myself to feel any guilt. Although, passing out on the living room floor isn't an experience many people would count themselves lucky to have.

I get to my feet, swaying slightly, and go to rinse the fuzzy feeling out of my mouth. I am in dire need of a toothbrush because it tastes like I ate so much ass last night. As I brush my teeth for the second time, I hear my phone go off mid-brush, so I rinse quickly and stride to my phone.

"Reeves," I bite out.

"Mr. Reeves, this is Officer Stanley with the St. Louis Police

Department. We've apprehended the young woman believed to have stolen your wallet and assaulted an officer. We're going to need you to come to the station and identify her. Unfortunately, your wallet wasn't recovered but she had over four hundred dollars on her, which I'm assuming is yours."

"Are you sure she doesn't have my wallet, or has she said where she stashed it?" I ask hurriedly. This is both good news and bad news.

"We're sure, sir, but we're holding her until you identify her. We'll book her after you file formal charges, and we'll question her more then," he says.

"I'll be there as soon as I can."

Exhausted, I look longingly to my Keurig but decide I don't have time, and instead, head to my bedroom to dress, cursing the beautiful thief who's making my life harder than it already was, unbelievably. It's like the universe doesn't want me to find my niece because I've encountered setback after setback, and I'm done playing this game. I'm getting her back, by any means necessary. If Miss Pickpocket knows what's good for her, she'll talk. Because, while I won't hurt a woman, with the charges about to be leveled against her, I can send her to jail for a while. I'm hoping the thought of that puts the fear of God into the little vixen.

I shove my legs into slacks and put on my boots as I call a driver to pick me up from my apartment. As I start to leave, I breathe deeply because I have a feeling this upcoming encounter is going to test my already thin patience. I'm thankful I took time off work to search for Cammie but my patience the last few months isn't what it used to be. My phone vibrates in my pocket, startling me out of my thoughts.

"Ryan," I bark. "I need you to get me in to talk to the girl who stole my wallet. I need a one-on-one. St. Louis P.D. has her in one of their holding cells." Of course, all I hear is laughter; this dude is all about getting his giggles in. Ass.

My driver finally rings the buzzer and I rub my temples one more time before exiting my apartment. The ride down the elevator has my head pounding with the lowering of each floor. This hangover might be what kills me, and if it isn't, then it's going to be the little minx who stole my wallet. My life just keeps getting more and more complicated by the day.

SIX

ZAYDRA

BEING ARRESTED AND BOOKED IS ABOUT AS FUN AS IT sounds. I'm also pretty positive I have frostbite on the tip of my nose, which would definitely add insult to injury. I'm currently in a large holding cell with seven other women. At least three of them are prostitutes, but to be fair, the other four are tweakers. One of the prostitutes is talking to herself. Crazy people are attracted to me—they always have been, thanks to my messed-up family—but I didn't expect her to make her way over to my bench and plop down. She turns her pretty face towards me, and I can't help but notice how gorgeous she is, with honey-colored hair and chocolate brown eyes. Too bad she's got a few screws loose.

"Hiya, I hope I'm not bothering you. I just wanted to come ask you if you would switch tits with me?" she says, and I blink at her as I tilt my head to the left. "Mine aren't nearly as great as yours, not that I'm a lesbian, mind you. Your rack is just pretty hard to miss, or look away from. So, what do you say... tradesies?"

I just stare at her as if she grew an extra head.

"Oh no, is it one of those, 'The wheels are spinning but the hamster is dead,' things with you?" she asks, while rotating one finger in a circle by her ear. I was in the process of scooting away from this crazy girl, but I stop to glare at her.

"Did you just call me an idiot? Did I just get called an idiot by a *prostitute?*" I exclaim, both to her and myself.

She starts speaking animatedly. "Oh! She talks! I'm sure you're not an idiot. You just weren't talking to me, and I needed a reaction, somebody to talk to preferably, or I'm going to go crazy in here." Crazy. Nailed it. I watch, fascinated, as she continues her speech. "Also, my name is Amber and I'm not a prostitute, or at least, not yet. You would be surprised how hard it is to pick up a man in St. Louis because they're all cops. No joke, I've been trying to get my first paying customer for months, but I've been busted sixteen times. Stripping doesn't pay the bills anymore, and I needed extra money, but I keep picking cops. Maybe I have a type? What do you think?" she asks, turning her brown doe eyes on me, as if she's staring into my soul. She has a way too intelligent set of eyes to be who she claims.

I don't have any idea what to make of this girl. A stripper-slash-failing prostitute, sitting with a pickpocket in a jail cell. We're either the beginning of a bad joke or an even worse porno. She's sitting primly on a bench in jail, surrounded by tweakers and prostitutes, wearing seven-inch stilettos in a tiny pink dress, and she's trying to make friends. My life just got weirder and I'm strangely okay with this new development. I take a deep breath.

"I'm Zaydra, and I don't think tit swaps are possible—not in this place, certainly—but how do you get busted *sixteen* times trying to prostitute yourself? There are plenty of men on every corner who proposition girls for sex every day. Most would probably be willing to pay for it."

"Zaydra is such a pretty name. So exotic, you'd make a killing as a stripper off that name alone, but I digress. Names can be moneymakers, I should know. I won't go with any of those nasty men on the street, that's how you get Gonoherpachlasyphi-lAIDS, don't you know? I go for the clean-cut guys, in nicer clothes, that approach me without catcalling or being forceful. They look like money and are respectful," she states smugly.

"Gonachla-what? Never mind, don't tell me. Amber, you realize you just described ninety-eight percent of undercover police officers in St. Louis, right? That's probably why you're getting caught," I reply with raised brows.

She looks bewildered for about three seconds before she laughs and sticks out her hand to me. "Amber Renee James, and you, Zaydra, have just taught me one thing I needed to know— who to stay away from. I'm in here for Solicitation, or in my case, Attempted Solicitation. What about you, sweets?"

I grin at the crazy, sweet girl and shake her hand. "Zaydra Jane Miller, Pickpocket extraordinaire at your service. I lifted a wallet off the most mouthwatering man I've ever seen last night, and then I assaulted a police officer, but he pulled my hair and didn't buy me dinner first," I find myself saying.

She grins, falters, and cups her boobs, then exhales noisily and says, "Oh good, you didn't steal my stripping money."

This girl. She's making me go full white girl, I can't even. I tip my head back and laugh heartily until she starts giggling. At that moment, the cell door smacks open with a *clang*, and every lady in the cell, including me, is mesmerized by the delicious sight in front of us. This man is sex on a stick in a three-piece suit, with an aura of danger surrounding him.

"Detective Stone," I hear Amber hiss. "You may kindly leave us all alone, and go fuck yourself."

I turn to look at her incredulously. I'm snarky, but I don't have an extended jail stay wish.

The beautiful man grins devilishly at her, and says, "Amber, I'm not surprised to see you in here. Still can't find any takers on your attempts at solicitation? You really should give that up. Maybe if you go back to church, you'll find your true calling, as a nun, because obviously no one wants to have sex with you, paid or not." This verbal sparring has got to be foreplay, but Amber's face is getting redder by the minute. Without warning, she shoots to her feet and stalks towards him. I'm pretty sure she's going to crush his balls.

"Why, you sanctimonious bastard. Just because you arrested me on my first attempt doesn't mean I haven't succeeded. I get plenty of takers and they pay top dollar for my Grade A magic —" she rants, but he shushes her.

"I know you're not successful because I have a whole team of guys following you, and I know you've failed, what, seventeen times? Or is it eighteen now? Besides, I'm not here for you. I'm here for her." He points straight at me.

At the same time, I'm thinking, *Shit*, Amber mutters, "Sixteen, you dick."

Detective Stone and everyone, including myself, laugh. That is, until he beckons me forward and says, "Come on. You've got interrogation and a line-up, ma'am."

I haul myself up and shuffle forward, trying to make myself look innocent. He just laughs softly and takes me by the arm. As the door shuts and a lock clicks into place, my eyes connect with Amber's. The look she gives me is silently telling me good luck. With one last vulgar gesture to the man beside me, she waves at me sadly.

Detective Stone leads me forward by my arm, bringing me to a gray door, which swings open and shows Mr. I Want To Sit On Your Face. He looks angry as hell. I gulp as I'm placed in my seat, feeling like I've bitten off a little more than I can chew.

He rasps, "So why don't you tell me why the hell you robbed me, and where the fuck my wallet is?"

Shit. Maybe I should have stayed in the jail cell with the hookers and tweakers.

SEVEN

COLLIN

As soon as the words are out of my mouth, I want to snatch them back. But I'm hungover as hell, angry, and in a sardine can of a room, trying to get this girl to tell me the location of the information that could be my niece's saving grace. The little thief gets an indignant look on her face. She says nothing but at the same time glares at me with more than a little heat, and I feel my dick start to harden, which only pisses me off. I try a different route.

"I just need my wallet back. I won't press charges if you tell me where it is, and I get it back safely," I say in a low voice, almost seductive, while staring into her wide green eyes.

"I didn't steal your damn wallet, so I have absolutely no idea what you could be talking about. The only things I happen to be guilty of are tripping into the wrong man—which happens to be you, genius—being poor, and running from a cop whose only purpose in life seemed to be shouting at me," she snaps indignantly.

She starts to thrum her fingers against the cold metal interrogation table, like she's impatient, as though she has somewhere else to be. I run my hands through my hair, feeling my fury rising. I lean across the small metal table towards her.

"I know you stole my wallet. You were the only one who got close enough, who I was more preoccupied in looking at, to feel you lift it from me. I don't want to cause you to stay in jail, but I will willingly tell these fine policemen that you were the one whole stole from me. And your pretty ass will stay in jail for a while, at least until you go to court," I nearly shout at her. As soon as I mention court, she turns white. I know I've spooked her, I just don't know why.

"What's your name, sweetheart? I don't want to keep making threats to a wisp of a girl without at least knowing your name," I drawl out, grinning at her.

"Now, Mr. Reeves, don't be hasty. I know I can help you figure out who stole from you. I know it wasn't me, and you know I don't belong in jail," she stutters.

She wets her lips with her tongue and I'm momentarily distracted by that plump fucking mouth again. I keep picturing my cock sliding between those lips until I hit the back of her throat. I shake myself out of my daydream when I notice I'm leaning towards her, and she seems to be leaning in to me as well.

I'm about to call her out on her ability to help me find this other "thief," when I stop cold. I tilt my head at the beautiful woman across from me. "I never told you my name, and I know Detective Stone didn't either. So how is it you know who I am, if you didn't steal my wallet?" I grit out.

She blinks at me, then panic skitters across her face before it settles into a cool mask of polite indifference. I know I have her now, though, and I grin triumphantly.

EIGHT

ZAYDRA

SHIT, SHIT, SHIT. WAY TO GIVE MYSELF AWAY. I'M AN accomplished pickpocket, not an accomplished liar. I can feel my stomach in my throat from the anxiety of having to lie to this man. I need a break from his intense stare, so I slide my gaze away from his and take in my surroundings.

One exit, back where Detective Stone is standing, all stoic, like that's his job. I'm in a tiny ass gray room, with one overhead light, a mirror on my right, and the stainless-steel table with the man across from me. Nothing I can remotely focus on other than him. I blink tiredly at the fluorescent light cascading over us, and decide fuck it I can't fight anymore. My energy is now completely gone and I feel my shoulders slump a little more.

"You might as well go ahead and press charges. Yes, I took your wallet, but I don't have it anymore. I tossed it in the trash, with all but the five hundred I borrowed from it." I don't know how I'm going to get out of court. If I go, and my name gets published, he will most definitely find me. I start to shake with the idea of him bringing me back. I won't go back to that life. I hate the icy terror that flows through my veins at the thought.

"A man like you can get another wallet, I.D., and credit cards with a snap of your fingers. I'll give most of the money back, well, Officer Sparky will. He took it from me when I came in. I don't get what's so important about that stupid wallet. You only had five hundred bucks and a slip of paper, it's not like it was thousands or even had family photos," I finish, and then sigh audibly.

His hand flies to mine. "Slip of paper? You saw it? Did you take it too? Please tell me you have it! I couldn't give two fucks about the rest. Tell me you have that paper!" he exclaims, so loudly I flinch. The unimportant slip of paper I had thrown away first, that was what he wanted? A plan starts to form in my brain, and I silently thank God for the one thing I had been born with that I've always hated.

"I don't have your paper, but I did look at it, and one thing I do have that you might find handy, is an eidetic memory. My photographic memory won't let me forget anything I've seen. So, if you get me out of here, and out of the charges I have against me, *all* of them, I'll tell you what I saw on that paper," I say, then grin, like I'm not shaking like a leaf inside.

"We both know that a photographic memory is a crock of shit. It's never been proven, Collin, she's bluffing. Let me take her back to the holding cell, we'll find Cammie another way," Detective Stone says.

I whip around to face him, pinning him with a glare, before I turn back to Collin, who looks extremely doubtful. I can almost feel my freedom slipping away, thanks to Detective AssHat. I refrain from the urge to give him the same vulgar hand gesture Amber did and decide to prove myself instead.

"Collin Anderson Reeves, born September 20, 1989, six foot four, two hundred fifteen pounds. Brown hair, blue eyes, lives at 11542 Central West End, Apartment 400, St. Louis, 63108. Oh, and he's an organ donor. In your photo, you had your hair parted to the right and a couple of strands fell into your left eye. You had the beginnings of a smirk as well," I spit out quickly.

He *would* live in the wealthiest area of St. Louis. I settle back and wait because I'm not going to give up the only collateral I have to get out of jail. Especially when I know the trash would be long gone by now. I smile at Collin slightly and hold his gaze. He would crack, I just knew it.

He turns to Detective Stone and speaks after a few long minutes. "We have to get her out of here, Ryan. She obviously can help me, you and I both know I need this information. I'll take her to my apartment, and you handle getting the charges dropped." He rises to his full height, and strides to me, although when he towers over me like this, I love it in the most twisted way possible. "You better be telling the truth, little girl, because there is a life riding on the information that you supposedly have in your head," he says softly.

I smile sweetly up at him, because I know he's my ticket out of here. "Zaydra Miller, at your service, Mr. Reeves."

NINE

COLLIN

IT TAKES ABOUT AN HOUR TO GET OFFICER STANLEY TO
agree to drop all the charges. Only after Zaydra apologized to
him and promised him it would never happen again did he
finally relent. As we started to walk out the door to the town car
I had waiting, Zaydra turns and says, "Don't worry, Officer
Sparky, a lot of men get bested by a girl. Remember to ice your
face tonight."

Then she blows him a kiss and waltzes outside. His face
grows dangerously red, and I just give him a helpless shrug and
follow her out. This girl, what the fuck am I supposed to do
with her?

My driver had already opened the door for her, and as I slide
in beside her, I say, "What the fuck was that? Are you trying to
go back to jail before we even leave the precinct?"

She bites her lip and then looks up at me through her lashes
as she leans back against the supple leather seat. When I remain
stoic against her "come hither" look, she blows out a breath and
glares at me.

"Relax, big man, I'm with you now. He's not going to arrest
me, and I owed him the last bit of snark for pushing my face
into the snow and ice outside a coffee shop, where everyone and

their mother could see. Come on, Collin, think of the children!" she says, with mock horror in her sweet voice.

I looked at her, exasperated, and then just shake my head. This was going to be one hell of a long car ride to my apartment. Thirty minutes of pure torture, and that's if I'm lucky and traffic decides to cooperate.

"Can you please just tell me what the paper said? I don't really have any more time to waste here. Like I said earlier, a life depends on it," I ask her. I feel like I'm whining, but I need this information. Collette needs this information. But most importantly, Cammie, my sweet, gangly, auburn-haired, freckle-faced niece, needs this information. I can't lose hope in finding her; I will not leave her to be used by a trafficking ring. She will be alive, and I will find her.

She must see the desperation on my face because she says quietly, "I will tell you everything I saw on the paper as soon as we get to your place and I eat something. I haven't eaten in three days, and I honestly can only focus on that right now. I realize this is important, but I wouldn't have stolen your wallet if I thought I was going to make it another day without food. Please."

My heart stumbles and lurches when I realize she's not lying. I hate the protective feeling it brings out in me, but I understand why she's not in a hurry to tell me. She thinks I'm going to kick her back out on the street once I know. The thought had occurred to me—after all, she *did* steal from me—but now I can't imagine doing that to her, and it has nothing to do with the fact I'm wildly attracted to her and her snarkiness. Okay, maybe it has a little to do with it.

I need to build up the walls around myself a little better because I can feel the ice in my blood that I've relied on for far too long start to melt. My gaze slides to the slight woman next to me, and I see her fight to stay awake. She intermittently jerks herself awake and glares at me. I pretend to shut my eyes to give her some semblance of comfort being in a car with a stranger while she is obviously exhausted. My eyes come open just as her eyelids start to flutter and she quietly falls asleep. Her breathing evens out, and her silky dark hair falls into her face. I wasn't done admiring, so I reach over to softly brush the strands away, and her eyes pop open, looking wild. Her fist shoots out, and I dodge it only because of all of the training I've religiously stuck to. I grab her fist before she can try to sock me again.

"Zaydra, calm down. I won't touch you again. I didn't mean to just then; it was an unconscious move on my part. I'm sorry." I inwardly cringe at how much I sound like a creep.

She scoots as far away from me as she can and grumbles something that sounds suspiciously like, "Ted Bundy was attractive and charming too," and then I hear, "Bet he has ear hair. Yeah, really long ear hair," and she falls asleep again with a slight smile.

I'm stupefied. She compares me to a serial killer and then insults my personal hygiene? I shake my head and catch myself checking my ears. Fuck, I need a drink. And a shower. And I need to stop mentally planning my next trip to the barber shop to get rid of all excess hair I have. I scowl the whole way home.

TEN

ZAYDRA

I JERK MYSELF AWAKE AS I FEEL THE CAR COME TO A STOP. I look over at Collin and see him talking quietly into his phone, but I can't catch what he's saying because of the sleep still fogging my brain. He finishes his call as the driver opens the door for us, then exits the car, and looks back at me.

"I don't have all day, Ms. Miller, so if you want your food, I suggest you hurry up."

Woah, Sir Douche Canoe, who pissed in your Wheaties from our conversation in the car to now? I can feel my face settle into my resting bitch "I smelled something bad" face. He's lucky I'm this hungry because I know better than to follow a stranger into a place I don't know, attractive or not. The only reason I got into the car with him in the first place was because I was so desperate to get away from that precinct filled with people who could ruin all the hiding I've done and everything I've worked so hard to get away from by showcasing where I am. If he tries something, I'm going to drop him like a sack of potatoes. I hope. The bigger they are, the harder they fall, right?

The building we're about to enter is obviously new. It has a doorman and is swanky as hell. As we enter, the opulence of the place is almost overwhelming. Everything is shiny and I become distinctly aware of how dirty and out of place I actually am. Collin is striding for the elevator before I even get a chance to get my bearings, so I quickly shuffle after him. I'm feeling a little too much like an obedient dog, so I say, "Who do I have to blow to get a place here? Because frankly, I feel like Julia Roberts in *Pretty Woman* up in this bitch."

I obviously mean it as a joke and to lighten the mood, but I see his eyes darken and he stares at me for about a minute.

"I own this building, if that's what you're asking, but as tempting as that vulgar offer is, I'd rather know what was on the fucking piece of paper."

I can see he's losing patience and I know it's not smart to poke the bear. I swear, I usually have a sense of self-preservation, but I'm pretty sure that went out the window when I set eyes on this man. "Well, who did you have to blow to own this place?"

It's like a car accident in slow motion and I'm pretty sure my foot in my mouth might be a disease that keeps recurring in me. I see him open his mouth, then close it again, and I swear this is the longest wait ever for the elevator. Finally, as I'm sure he's about to rip me a new one, the elevator dings, and I have been quite literally saved by the bell. I exhale and dart into the open elevator, then turn and give him a megawatt smile. He stalks on to the elevator, shaking his head and looking mostly exasperated.

"How many people live in this building? There have to be twelve floors, and why do you live on the fourth floor if you own this building?" I ask.

"There are ten renters other than myself, and the first floor is the only floor that has multiple apartments strictly for staff. The rest of the floors are entire apartments. I have the fourth-floor apartment because I'm not the best with heights, so I have no need for a penthouse apartment. Four stories is almost too high as it is," he says, and stares stoically at the elevator numbers as they rise. As if he didn't just give me a peek of the vulnerable man underneath the sex-on-a-stick persona.

Somehow, a common fear like that just makes him seem

more human to me, and weirdly puts me more at ease. The elevator reaches the fourth floor, but doesn't open, so I see him pull out a key and insert it into the slot by the "4" button on the panel. As soon as he turns the key, the doors open into a huge living area.

My mouth drops open, and he shakes his head and strides out. As he turns and motions for me to follow, I finally come out of my stupor and hurry out, but it's been long enough. As soon as I start out of the elevator, the doors begin to close and catch my foot. Collin has a look of horror on his face as I feel myself go down. When I hit my face on the floor, you could hear a pin drop before my loud exclamation of, "*Balls*!"

Not my proudest moment, but I've certainly been in worse situations than that. I lay there for a good minute before I roll over and blink up at the dark angel that is Collin, as he stares down at me, obviously struggling not to laugh. "Help me up, please, you big brute!" I crankily bite out.

He leans down and scoops me up into his arms, then walks over to the day bar area and sets me down on a stool.

"I'd rather you not bleed on the marble floors. My cleaning lady would have my ass, so if you could refrain from any more falls, that would be great. Also, if you could refrain from shouting about balls loud enough for my neighbors above and below to hear, that would also be appreciated. I wouldn't want them to think I have a woman in here that has a kinky ball fetish," he says, humor lacing his tone.

I can feel my face heat. He's looking at me with amusement in his eyes, so I do the most adult thing I can. I sniff daintily, and then stick my tongue out at him. He finally loses it and laughs deeply, which might be one of the sexiest things I've ever heard. Before I can say anything else, he pulls out his phone and I hear him tell someone, whom I'm assuming is the manager of this joint, that he needs enough takeout food to feed an army. Then he hangs up.

The power of this man makes my panties damp; just the air

of authority around him is sexy. He tells me to wait where I am for a moment and disappears. I use this opportunity to look around his apartment, which is one of those places where you can just *feel* the money in this place. Matching furniture, a huge television, and a large window with what looks like a balcony overlooking the city in the living room. The kitchen is so modern and updated and so large, I'm pretty sure a chef or baker would orgasm on sight.

He returns after about five minutes with clothes in his hands. "I figured you might want to change into something that's clean and dry. I can show you to the bathroom, if you want to shower and change before the food arrives."

The amount of kindness in this man for someone who stole from him and is withholding information he's obviously desperate for, takes my breath away. I silently grab the clothes and let him lead me halfway down the hall, to the most beautiful bathroom I've ever seen.

ELEVEN

COLLIN

WHEN SHE'S SILENT, IT'S HARD FOR ME TO REMEMBER I'M supposed to be mad at her. She just looks so tiny and tired. I hear the shower turn on and I start to pace in the living room. I know I need to push for the information. There's nothing I care about more than Cammie, and I can't help but worry and pray she's still alive. I shouldn't have waited to read the note, but the fucking tweaker informant assured me I was being watched, and that I needed to wait until I was home and alone. I hate myself in this moment because I can feel Cammie slipping further and further away.

The hate these men have for me is out of control, and if Cammie isn't dead or sold, it won't be too much longer—I know that, realistically. I have to lie to Collette and tell her she's going to be fine, but when I get her back, she might never be the same. I sit on the couch and put my head in my hands, feeling more desolate than I have in a while, because I'm finally letting myself realize the truth. No matter what, I'm not giving up hope, though. I can't, because Collette is counting on me. Hell, Cammie is counting on me.

I hear a noise and look up, locking eyes with Zaydra. With her wet hair, and wearing my clothes, I almost forget my own name. She's so beautiful it hurts, and our eyes stay locked until the elevator buzzer rings.

I tip the doorman for our food, and then turn to find her already seated where I had originally placed her. "Do you need help?" she asks, but I just wave her offer away and make my way around the kitchen.

I get everything organized and make her a heaping plate of food, then set it in front of her. Her eyes light up with such pleasure that my cock jerks, and she looks up and says, "Thank you, Chinese is one of my favorites," with so much gratitude, like I just handed her the keys to my apartment rather than a simple meal.

This girl…this girl could be the death of me. Her sweet and sassy are just the perfect combination, and instead of saying, "You're welcome," like a gentleman, I grunt at her, like a Neanderthal. Thankfully, she's so engrossed with her food, she doesn't notice. I start in on my own plate.

"So, before I give you the information you're so obviously desperate for, I would like to know why it's important. You said a life was on the line, and I would like you to explain that. Please," she says, after she's finished nearly half her meal.

I debate not telling her, because we both know it's none of her business, but she is obviously a nosy one, and I know she'll just refuse to tell me the information on the note if I don't. So, I swallow my last bite of food, and then take a deep breath.

"I should start at the beginning then," I start, then take another calming breath. "Three years ago, before I made my fortune, I was taking part in a classified mission as part of special ops. Not an unusual occurrence, but this one wasn't like other missions. This one was domestic, and it had to do with a pedophilic sex trafficking ring out of New Orleans. A senator's daughter had been snatched and the federal government sent us in, unofficially, to retrieve her." I paused the memory nearly drowning me.

"When we finally made them, we went in quietly, in the

dead of night, but when we got inside, things went to shit, very quickly. The girl was severely addicted to drugs and ran to her captor when we tried to rescue her. She ran through the building to his room. I'm not sure if it was Stockholm Syndrome or the drugs, but when he saw her, he smiled, and when he saw us, he smiled wider."

Zaydra leans closer, barely breathing as she listens.

"He held a gun to her head. It was myself and Detective Stone in the room, the other men were getting the other girls out. He was obviously the head of the ring. The girl was sobbing and I couldn't get a clear shot. He looked straight at me and pulled the trigger. Didn't try to negotiate or anything, just kills her and smiles at me, so I pull the trigger, and drop him. His name was Carlos Gonzales and his smile still haunts me." I take a steadying breath because the next part is much harder.

"I got out of the military after that. I couldn't forgive myself for letting that poor girl die. Ryan did as well, and he became a detective while I made my millions in private security and electronic deciphering. I was always good with computers but I was better at protecting people. I had a lot of wealthy clients. About two and a half years go by, and then six months ago, an article was published in the *New York Times* about me and my past, stating my net worth, but the pictures with it were the huge part. There was an old military picture, and a picture that contained my twin sister and her daughter."

"The next day, I received a phone call from my sister, Collette, saying she and my niece, Cammie, had had a fight, and Cammie took off to the mall with her friends, but that had been hours ago. She sounded worried, but I laughed it off and told her it was just Cammie being a teenager, and even if she had run away, that she would be back by morning, I was so sure of it." I exhale hard, wishing this story was finished. I wish like hell I had been a better brother and a better uncle and jumped into action right then.

"The next morning, Cammie still hadn't shown up, but

again, she's gone to friends' houses before and not called her mother until after noon. She has always been a late sleeper. It was at 12:30 that I received a note, which said, 'We grabbed her because you took him from us. We hope you enjoy spending your life knowing she's going to be drugged and used in every way possible. You'll never see her again, and know it's your fault.' It was signed one letter—J. The note contained a picture of my niece tied up. The new head, or heads, of the organization obviously recognized me from the pictures, and took the only thing important enough to me to drive me crazy."

"We haven't been able to get a single lead on their whereabouts, even using all of my military connections, or the computers at my fingertips. It's like they're ghosts. And the only lead I've had on her in six months, you threw out with my wallet. So, I need you to tell me what you know right now," I grit out.

She puts her fork down silently, and looks me straight in the eye. "The note said, 'She's alive, last known whereabouts, the Warehouse District, New Orleans. The leader loves the Camisole.' It didn't make sense, so I tossed it. I thought maybe you were into some weird shit and I don't kink shame. And I'm sorry. But she is alive."

My heart drops and as my eyes close, I feel a single tear run down my cheek.

TWELVE

ZAYDRA

I SEE THE EMOTION ON HIS FACE AND THE TEAR THAT tracks down his cheek, and I'm regretting my decision to rob this man, or even keep this information from him as long as I did. If I had known, I wouldn't have, but I can't help but feeling as though fate brought us together. I feel his pain as if it were my own, and I'm determined to find this girl as well. I look down at my plate that still has food on it, but my appetite is gone, and I have a million questions. I don't want to push him when he's emotional. If I know anything about emotional men, it's that they can be extremely volatile. But I have to try.

"Is her full name Camisole?" I ask. He looks confused for a minute, and then he shakes his head.

"Her legal name has always been Cammie. Only I call her Camisole as a joke to her and her mother," he says dejectedly, and then sighs forcefully. "The only way the fucking people would have known that is from asking her, or hearing me call her that. Like they were watching her, or watching us together," he finishes angrily.

Before I can open my mouth to respond, he rises smoothly from the bar where we were eating. He starts to stalk away, but I quickly grab him by the arm and he turns with a snarl on me.

"We'll find her, Collin. She's alive, and she's much more valuable to them that way because they know it guts you. These men are sadistic, they want to inflict as much pain to you as possible. This is personal, I just can't figure out why. To most of these types of men, it has to be just about business. Personal vendettas get people killed," I say quietly.

I mean that more than he can ever know. I stare at him so intently, willing him to feel my conviction and sincerity, but I watch his gaze lower to my hand still gripping his bicep. I quickly let go and feel the temperature of the room jump a couple of degrees, as heat creeps up my face when his eyes lock with mine again. The attraction I have for him is out of control and frankly inappropriate in this situation. I wet my suddenly dry lips, and his eyes lock on my mouth.

His eyes darken with what I've only ever constituted with lust. I hope it's lust and not gas, because I don't think my female ego could take it. Although, maybe he's the type of man who gets gassy in stressful situations. Wouldn't that suck—

My thoughts are interrupted when he closes the distance and slams his mouth on mine in a forceful kiss. *Definitely not gassy,* I think, and I moan when he licks the seam of my lips until I let him in. His tongue duels softly with mine and I can feel myself trying to get closer to him, because it's the type of kiss that just makes me crave more. More of him, and more contact to ease the fire suddenly in my core. He deepens the kiss, and it makes me feel out of control. I rub my center on his jean-clad thigh that he's pushed between my legs. A jolt of pleasure goes through me, and I moan into his mouth. I should be afraid but there is no room for fear with passion like this making me go up in flames.

He suddenly springs away from me, breathing hard, leaving my body on fire and my nipples in hard points. I'm panting when he says, "We can't do this. Not when I have to find Cammie, and for fucking sure not after you stole from me."

I can't seem to get my brain to catch up, so I take a deep

breath. He's walking away quickly, as if he didn't just rock my world with a single kiss.

"I'm sorry, I'm so sorry," I whisper, and I genuinely am, even though I would for sure have starved without that money. In this moment, I wish things were different. That I led a different type of life, and I was a different type of woman for this dangerous broken man. I'm wanting things I have no hope of ever having, and I know I should leave this apartment and this man, but I can't bring myself to do it. I might not know Cammie personally, but I feel like her fate is now irrevocably intertwined with mine.

I hear him moving around in the next room, and I can hear his muffled voice as if he's talking to someone. I subconsciously move closer, creeping to the edge of the door that must be his study. It's cracked slightly and I can hear his voice louder, right on the other side of the door. I see him pacing the floor.

"She told me what it said, Ryan, and I believe her." He pauses before speaking again. "No, why would she lie? That doesn't make any sense, she can't exploit me for anything." Collin pauses again, then says, loudly, "Ryan! Just fucking listen to me! Cammie is alive, and she's in New Orleans. Back to where this fucking started."

He nods to whatever Ryan is saying on the other end, and I wish I could hear the other side of this conversation. Detective Stone obviously doesn't trust me, hell, *I* wouldn't trust me. My mind is brought back to the scene at hand as Collin continues, "She's somewhere in the Warehouse District, if they haven't moved her. The disgusting pricks know that I call her Camisole. They wanted me to hear this information. I don't know how I know but I know."

He pauses his incessant pacing as if listening and then says, "Ryan, fuck, of course I need a team of men. I'm definitely going in to get her. It might take a couple of weeks of reconnaissance, but I'm fucking getting her back." The anger in his tone is palpable, and I press my lips together before I try to say something to comfort him. He finishes his conversation with a tone softer than before. "Ryan, I can't ask you to take that much time off your job, but I am doing this, with or without you."

He ends the call and turns so his back is to the door. I'm about to slip away when I hear, "Zaydra, it's not polite to eavesdrop on private conversations. The least you could do is join me."

Busted. I somehow momentarily forgot Collin was Special Forces, so no matter how quiet I was, he most likely heard me. I slink into the room, feeling like a chastised child. When I'm standing a few feet behind him, he turns and his impossibly handsome face looks severe. His eyebrows are furrowed, giving the impression of anger mixed with exhaustion. He must see my cringe because he smiles in a ferocious way, showing his straight white teeth. I'm not sure if he wants to kiss me or shake me by this point.

"Why are you a badass one moment, and a cowering girl the next?" he muses out loud. I feel my shoulders stiffen as I stand tall.

"If you think I'm afraid of you, Collin, you are sorely mistaken. I've been afraid of one man my whole life, and you, sweetheart, are not him. So kindly eat a dick," I say sweetly, and his eyebrows shoot up. Before he can respond, I continue, "You can't use your niece as an excuse to be an ass, so don't eat just one dick. Eat a whole bag of them, big ones preferably."

Then, like a badass, I turn and exit the room. God, he riles me up so easily. I stomp to the living room and throw myself on his expensive furniture, silently giving a big middle finger to his decorator.

THIRTEEN

COLLIN

MY MOUTH DROPS OPEN AS SHE FLOUNCES OUT OF THE room, and all I'm left with is the subtle scent of cherries and vanilla, which is her unique scent, and my own embarrassment. I walk out of the room hot on her tail. I make it to the living room, finding her with her limbs thrown over the couch.

"Go ahead and make yourself comfortable," I mutter under my breath. I sit on the loveseat, as far from the little vixen as I can possibly get without leaving the room. She looks over at me with those big, green eyes, and all I want to do is kiss her again as I sink inside her wet heat. I shake my head to dispel those thoughts and she smirks at me, like she knows what I'm thinking, and I feel my cock harden. I can't adjust myself without her seeing me, so I just raise my chin at her, daring her to say something. She did, after all, just tell me to eat a bag of dicks. She's lucky I don't make her choke on mine.

She suddenly sits up and looks at me seriously. "What's our plan for getting Cammie back?" she asks, and I stare at her incredulously. She can't think she has any place near this situation. I'm literally at a loss for words.

"*Our* plan?" I say as my eyebrows shoot up to my hairline.

"Yes, our plan. Like it or not, I'm involved, and I have an

advantage most of the men on your 'team' don't have. I have an eidetic memory, and I lived in New Orleans for a few weeks, so I can give you an accurate map of the Warehouse District, because that's where I stayed. Including the sewers," she says smugly.

I can feel my heart start to pound, because honestly, she's right—that alone would cut the recon time in half. We went in last time with inside information that wasn't quite accurate, which ended up causing the rescue mission to go to shit. I feel crazy because I'm actually contemplating bringing her with us, a pickpocket, who stole from me. Eidetic memory or not, I don't know if I can trust her. That, and the fact I can't go two minutes without thinking about taking out my frustration on her pussy, and pounding into her until we both come.

"I don't know if that's a good idea. I'm not going to lie to you, that would be handy as hell to have on this mission, but I don't trust you. After all, you did steal from me. And I can't afford to gamble Cammie's life on whether or not you feel like helping me or stealing from me again," I say with a stoic face, feeling ice drip into my tone. The rage and the helplessness of the situation threaten to overwhelm again.

She looks at me knowingly, then stands suddenly and comes over to where I'm sitting and takes the seat next to me. She stares straight into my eyes for a minute, visibly shudders, then grabs my hand and squeezes it.

"You have absolutely no reason to trust me, but I feel like it was fate that we came into each other's lives when we did. I feel like I'm supposed to help you, to help Cammie. Maybe this is a little bit of my redemption, but regardless, I genuinely want to help her. I know what going through hell by the hands of men feels like, and if I can help save one girl from it, I would move heaven and earth to do so."

I hear the sincerity in her voice, and it makes me fall half in love with this beautiful, broken girl right there on my loveseat, while she's wearing my clothes and holding my hand. It's enough to nearly forget everything that happened to bring us to this moment.

"Okay, you can come," I say after a long moment of silence, more moved by her words than I care to admit. "But you follow my rules, *and* you play nice with the others. No stealing, and for fuck's sake, don't tell anyone to eat a bag of dicks."

She smiles brilliantly at me, and I can't help but feel like I just made a deal with the devil. A beautiful tiny devil named Zaydra. I blow out my breath heartily and she laughs lightly. Just when I thought this headache was going away, it manifests itself into human form.

FOURTEEN

ZAYDRA

After the intense talk on the couch, like the gentleman he is, Collin shows me to the guest bedroom for me to get some much-needed sleep. I step through the doorway into a beautiful gray room with a queen-sized bed in the middle of the room. The room is fairly large and has some of the plushest white carpet I've ever felt. I'm almost sad I don't have to sleep on the floor tonight, if not just to experience this carpet.

"Will this do for you tonight, milady?" Collin says with an amused smirk. He must have seen the wonderment on my face at actually having a safe place to sleep.

I cock a hip and give him a mischievous smile. "Well, it's no Four Seasons, but it'll do just this once. As long as you have a cabana boy in a thong come and fluff my pillows, who will leave me a mint, we'll be just fine."

He lets out a laugh that seems to surprise even him, and shakes his head at me before turning to leave. Two steps from the door, he turns and strides back over to me. He grips me by my upper arms.

Collin surprises me by kissing me softly on the forehead, and then whispers, "Thank you for being the type of outrageous and sweet that I need in my life right now. Thank you for just wanting to help, even when you weren't sure if I was going to throw you out on the street after. Just…thank you. If you need anything, I'm right down the hall."

Then, just as abruptly, he releases me and walks out of the bedroom, leaving me alone with my thoughts. Making me wonder, for the first time in a long time, if maybe, just maybe, not all men were evil in their core. Maybe, just maybe, I could trust this one.

I take a minute and do my hygiene activities with the toiletries his guest en suite bathroom provided. Then I make my way over to the bed and sink down into it for the first time. I may have let out a tiny moan, or I may have shouted, "Fuck, this is the tits." I'll never tell, but feeling this bed—rather, this cloud made from an angel's wings—no one would blame me.

I savor the feeling of comfort and security, more so than I've experienced in a long time. The last thought I have before my mind blissfully slips away into dreamland is that I'm infinitely glad I don't have to sleep somewhere without heat or on the hard ground tonight. I'm sure I drift off with a smile on my face, and I pray my subconscious doesn't kick me in the teeth and ruin this perfect moment.

FIFTEEN

COLLIN

I'M AWAKENED AROUND ONE IN THE MORNING TO A CHOKED cry coming from my guest bedroom down the hall. I spring up in bed, unaware of the cause of the sound, before I remember I have a certain female guest in that room. Normally, I would check on someone, but it was one cry and we don't know each other well enough to—

A shrill shriek has me bolting from my bed, down the hall to the guest room. I rip open the door, only to see Zaydra sitting up and screeching at the ceiling, watching something with unseeing eyes. She's flinging her head side to side, as if being struck. It's way too much for me, so I climb into the bed and rub up and down her arms. "Zaydra, Zaydra, you're safe, you're safe! Whatever it is can't hurt you, I have you."

I go through this mantra three times before she calms down. Her eyes close and then reopen with awareness. She seems to understand what she had been awakened from was a nightmare, just a nightmare, but that doesn't stop her from crawling into my lap and wrapping her arms around me, sobbing loudly. It makes me want to kill whatever, or whoever, it was that had hurt her this badly.

I rub circles on her back while she cries softly, just wanting to offer comfort, and keep repeatedly telling her she's safe. All she does is nod and continue to softly sob, but it's breaking my heart. Finally, I pull back to look at her, and those deep green eyes wet with tears are so haunted, I have to ask.

"Zaydra, who hurt you? Why do you look so haunted, why are the nightmares so bad? I just want to help you," I say softly, genuinely wanting to help this beautiful, broken girl. She stares at me for a full minute until her tears slowly subside, and she smiles at me sadly.

"Just a past I can never seem to escape. No matter how far I run, it always seems to be there to remind me that I'm not good and I don't deserve this kindness that you're bestowing on me," she replies delicately, as if she is a moment from shattering.

Her look turns to a shuttered one as she takes in my body. In my rush to get to her, I forgot I was only in boxer briefs. She wets her lips, and I feel heat surge to my dick. He doesn't care that this moment is inappropriate for anything but comfort. My dick goes to half-mast just from her running her tongue along her lips, and then my brain decides to take in that she's only wearing the thin shirt I gave her. I can see her nipples poking through at me, begging for my mouth on them. I discretely adjust my now fully-hard dick, which I can't possibly hide in these boxer briefs.

"You know what you could do to help me, though, Collin?" she says suddenly, shifting closer. All of a sudden, she is straddling me. I look up at her, and I'm dazed, wondering how she got me on my back. She leans down and whispers, "You can help me forget. Please, just help me forget for tonight."

Slowly, she starts to rock her wet core back and forth on my achingly hard cock, soaking the material of my boxer briefs, and the heat from her pussy right on top of my dick makes me groan.

"You want to be fucked, baby? I'm not a sweet nothings type of man, but if you need me to fuck you until you forget everything but the feel of my hard cock sliding in and out of your tight little pussy, I can do that. Is that what you want, baby?" I growl out, as I thrust against her, then grip her hips tightly to grind that wet pussy against my dick.

I hear her whimper, and bring her face to mine to catch her plush lips for a punishing kiss. Only after my lungs start to ache for air do I break the kiss, and as I start to massage her ample tits with my large hands, I feel her legs tighten around my hips.

"Do you need to come, baby, is that what you need? You want to get off just rubbing your clit on my clothed dick?" I squeeze her hips and use them as leverage to rub her against my dick faster. Her breath turns into pants and I know she's so close to coming already, but I need to be the one to get her off, and not just with this teenage dry humping. So, I flip her over, push up her t shirt, and kiss my way down her stomach until I get to the small triangle of neatly-trimmed hair that covers her pussy.

I use my thumb and forefinger to open her pussy lips so I can see her gorgeous pink slit, glistening, and her clit, red and engorged, and I blow lightly. Her hips start to buck from the sensations. I bring my mouth down fully and take my first full lick. She tastes a little sweet and salty, with a certain musk that keeps my dick hard, and it has precum leaking from the tip of my dick. I could eat her forever, she tastes that fucking good.

As soon as I flick her clit with my tongue, I thrust two fingers into her tight cunt, and she fucking goes off like a fire-cracker. She screams with the intensity of her orgasm, and it gets me so worked up, I almost come from watching her. Only from sheer willpower do I stave off my own orgasm. I barely stop myself from coming in my boxer briefs like a fourteen-year-old seeing his first pair of tits.

When Zaydra reopens her eyes to look up at me, she splays her legs open wider and leans up slightly to rip off the t shirt she was wearing. She gives me the sexiest "come hither" smile I've ever seen. Then, she rocks my world when she says huskily, "Now that you've shown me what your mouth can do, don't follow it up with dick disappointment. Fuck me, make me forget anything but you. Please, Collin."

I position myself between her legs, but I jack my length just shy of her opening, and she whimpers. I lean over to grab a condom from the nightstand. Once I tear it open and roll it on, I continue to tease her clit with the head of my dick until she's gasping for breath, continually pleading with me to fuck her, begging me and telling me she'll be a good girl if I just fuck her. I have no idea how I've held back this long, but when she tells me that, I lodge my thick cock into her opening and slam home before she can draw her next breath.

It's like I've died and gone to heaven. I'm seeing stars, and feeling the tight hot grip of her pussy around my dick might kill me yet. I give her time to adjust to my size, but when she starts squirming, I take that as my cue to slowly slide my cock almost all the way out, and then slam back into her wet heat. Her pussy starts to clench around my dick, milking it. So greedy for cum, but I hold back.

I look down at the place where my dick is splitting her open, and then I look at her beautiful face, with her bedroom eyes focused on me. "Ask me, please, if I will fuck you, and tell me that you love it, like a good little girl, Zaydra," I rasp out as I steadily slide in and out of her heat at a slower rhythm. She makes a sound deep in her throat and scratches her nails down my back, which almost has me going off again, but I bite down on her neck to get her to stop. Licking the spot I bit, to soothe it, I grunt, "Say it, baby."

"Please, will you fuck me harder, Collin? Please fuck me, I love it, I'm so close. I need to come, please make me come. I'll be so good," she sobs out, and it's all I need.

I start fucking her with abandon, thrusting so hard the head-board starts to knock into the wall. Her tits are bouncing with each thrust, and I can feel my orgasm rushing to meet me head-on, so I wet my fingers and use them to pinch her clit lightly. It's just enough, and she screams my name as she comes hard enough her pussy clamps down on my dick so tightly, it triggers my orgasm.

"Zaydra. Oh, fuck," I groan. My last coherent thought is, she *would* have a goddamn magic pussy on top of everything else.

SIXTEEN

ZAYDRA

I COME AWAKE TO MY CLIT TINGLING. EARLY MORNING light is filtering through the window, and I look down to see Collin nuzzling his face in my tits. My nipples have since tightened to points, just from his warm breath on them. I can't believe I passed out after that earth-shattering orgasm. More to the point, I can't believe I slept with this man after only knowing him for one day.

My inner self is fist pumping and cringing at the same time, but fuck it, let's be honest—hashtag hoe life or no life. I deserve to have a sexual experience that doesn't make me cringe. I cannot invite any more intimacy into my life, so this is really the best I'm going to get. I just don't want to complicate things any more than I have for him. Lord knows he's been through enough, and I hate adding to the weight already on his shoulders.

My body jerks as his wet mouth closes over a tight nipple and when he starts to lightly suck, I'm pretty sure I see stars. His mouth is sending zings of pleasure from my tits to my core, and I'm getting wetter by the second. I let out a fairly loud moan and feel myself undulating underneath this bear of a man. He finally raises himself up to grin lazily down at me with lust darkening his eyes. In the early morning light, I get my first real good look at his body, and holy fuckballs, Batman, this man is stacked. He must eat pure protein and virgins for breakfast because he's got an eight pack and the glorious V leading to one of the biggest cocks I've seen not in porn.

I, however, am a shoulder girl, and his are tight with muscles and make my mouth water. I'd sit on his face just to be close to them. After he ate me like he was starving last night, I know it would be my favorite seat in the house.

His hand slides down my belly to part my thighs. He finds my wet, aching pussy, and gives my clit a light pinch, making me come off the bed. Collin thrusts two fingers in, stretching my tightness to the point it's almost painful with his thick fingers. He pumps his fingers into me three times, just enough where I can feel the tightening of my impending orgasm start in my belly.

Suddenly, he pulls his fingers from my pussy like the devil he is. My groan must sound pathetic, because he laughs huskily and brings his fingers first to his mouth to suck my juices off the first digit. His eyes darken and my pussy clenches as he brings the second finger to my mouth. I can smell my own arousal, and normally it would embarrass me, but at this point, I'm too turned on to care. I wrap my lips around the digit and suck it deep into my mouth, tasting myself and his own saltiness. I feel more wetness slip out of my pussy as he stares down at me with so much heat, I'm almost sure I can come just from him looking at me that way.

He grips his thick cock with his other hand, while his finger is still in my mouth. He finally pulls it from me with a slight grunt, and starts stroking himself, just to the sight of me. He leans over to grab a condom and fully sheaths himself. My clit tingles with anticipation as Collin takes the head of his dick and rubs it up and down my slit, coating himself with my wetness, and teasing me even more.

I'm so close to shattering with little to no stimulation, and am nearly to the point of begging. When our eyes lock, he slams into me and whispers, "Come for me, Zaydra."

And I do. My pussy clenches and my wetness gushes around his dick, making his thrusts slightly easier. My body and mind are in the stars, and so many sensations overwhelm my pussy and clit as he continues with his steady onslaught of thrusts. He suddenly rears back and slams into me harder, growling, "Again."

Without my permission, my body falls over the edge into a second orgasm, and I'm pretty sure I see God, and feel what heaven is like.

He's slamming his hips into me, hard and fast. My body has no time to recover before he's rubbing circles on my clit and my body is catapulted into another mind-blowing orgasm. I'm coming so hard I vaguely become aware of myself chanting, "Collin, Collin, fuck Collin."

As if hearing his name on my lips is his trigger, Collin's pace becomes erratic, and he thrusts into me twice more before growling out his release. I feel his dick harden even more inside me, and through the condom, I can feel the hot spurt of his cum marking me. His breathing is harsh on my neck and the sunlight in the room is becoming brighter. I'm safe, satisfied, and content, and this scares the hell out of me. My breath escapes me in heavy gusts.

Finally, after what feels like forever, Collin pulls out and rises to dispose of the condom. I get my first view of his spectacular ass, and I swear I'm thinking of switching to a religion that solely worships him as a deity. I send up a little prayer I won't wake up from this dream in the abandoned apartment in downtown St. Louis. It's such a nice dream.

I sit up and pull the blanket around my naked body, and wait for Collin to return from the bathroom, knowing it's imperative to talk about us fucking before we go on this rescue excursion. Five minutes pass, then eight. Finally, I rise from the bed, fully intent on checking on him, when he stalks out of the bathroom with a strained look on his face. He's about to ruin my nice post-sex glow, I just know it, even before he opens his mouth.

"Zaydra..." he begins, but I know what's coming so I cut him off.

"Don't, just don't." I shake my head. "I know what you're going to say. That it was a mistake, it can't happen again, especially not with your niece's life on the line. I understand, I get it, but please, don't say it. Message received, Captain Fucks-A-Lot." He simply stands there, his mouth slightly parted, and he looks so cute, I just mutter, "Dick." *That'll teach him.*

"Well, I was going to tell you about the genital herpes flare-up that I'm having, but you nailed the other thing I was thinking, so I guess I'll let it go," he finally replies drolly.

It's my turn for my mouth to hang open because, while I know he's joking, we didn't have the safe sex talk and I'm not trying to get infected by God of Sex over there. I shake my head and just glare at him, unimpressed. Then I do what I do best, I run away. Huffing, I rush around him into the bathroom and slam the door as hard as I can, and stick my tongue out at the closed door. While I know it's impractical to be upset at what he did and didn't say, I feel tears sting my eyes. Ugh, I hate being such a girl sometimes.

"*C'est la vie,*" I whisper to myself as I stare in the mirror. Some days, that's the only thing that keeps me going. It is what it is. I just have to continue to breathe through it.

SEVENTEEN

COLLIN

I'm slamming things around my kitchen, making breakfast, after thoroughly fucking up the first sexual encounters I've had in I don't know how many months. I'm angry she wasn't even a little clingier, how messed up is that? I barely know her, but the primal part of me has already claimed her as mine. I know, realistically, it's my way of dealing with stress, and the all-consuming attraction I feel towards Zaydra.

I can't afford to be distracted, though, and I almost want to tell her she can't come with me on this mission. But the logical part of my brain reminds me her memory will in fact come in handy, and that I need all the help I can get if I plan on taking on a completely deranged and dangerous sex trafficking ring on my own. I wipe my hand down my face to dispel my negative thoughts, and I feel her presence enter the room before I hear her. She can be ridiculously quiet when she wants to be.

"Do you need any help?" she asks from behind me, and I close my eyes at the sweetness of her tone.

It would be so easy to break this girl, but even easier for her to break me. Incapable of verbally responding, I shake my head no. I turn to give her the mug of coffee I brewed for her and I'm hit with her beauty, her innocence, once again. It steals the breath from my lungs when she shyly smiles up at me, and I feel like she has me by the balls. Maybe she *is* a witch, bewitching me until I lose all good reason and sense. She takes the mug and has a seat at the day bar, then proceeds to doctor the coffee with two creams and what must be a gallon of sugar. I cock my eyebrow at her, and she huffs, "What? I like things that are sweet."

I almost choke. *Me too, me too.*

After our omelets are finished, I set a plate in front of her and sit down with my own. She thanks me gratefully and digs in. I stare at her while she eats with gusto, like she doesn't know when her next meal will be. It makes me sad, dampening my own appetite. She finally looks up and grins at me sheepishly, shrugging her shoulders as if to say, "What're you gonna do?"

I finally dig into my own food, all the while wondering how someone like her becomes homeless, wishing like hell I could chase all her demons away for her. Knowing I can't, because my own are coming knocking. "Eat up and change, we leave within the hour. The team Detective Stone is putting together will meet us in New Orleans in two days' time. I figure we can get there early enough to do some slight reconnaissance of our own. With your memory and my training, we could very well sniff these men out quicker, I hope," I finally say.

She nods at me, with a slightly thoughtful look on her face. "Thank you for breakfast, I hope this won't be weird between us, especially if we're going to be alone together for the next two days. *And* doubly, especially since I can't help but want to sit on your face. But don't worry, I won't. It won't be like a surprise face-sitting attack from me, you don't have to worry about it. Fucking monkey balls, you make me nervous. Can you just stop staring at me like I have a third nipple, I ramble when I'm nervous, *okay*?!" Zaydra says.

I exhale, bewildered, and I can only hope and pray I survive the next forty-eight hours alone with her, then I pray my niece hangs on just a little longer. I'm coming, with the most unlikely of help, but I'm coming.

EIGHTEEN

ZAYDRA

I WAS SOMEWHAT SHOCKED HE CHOSE TO DRIVE US WHEN he could have called for a car, and that he seems at ease in jeans and a black Henley. This is the most relaxed I've seen him, with his right hand propped on the steering wheel of the black Range Rover we're currently traveling in, his Ray Bans propped on his calm face. He's not as uptight as I feared he would be, thank God. I don't know if I could survive the next ten hours in this car with General Grumbles-A-Lot.

In the silence, I find myself studying his strong profile. We haven't talked since we loaded up, but it's not an uncomfortable silence. I start noticing things about him I hadn't before, like the freckle on the right side of his neck, where the muscles flex and contract, and you can tell this strong, resilient man has the weight of the world on his shoulders. He sits slightly hunched forward, like he's squatting three hundred pounds. I know he's got more worries than he should, and I can't imagine what his sister must be feeling.

He reaches over and cranks the radio, disrupting my musing. All I hear is "The Sound of Silence" by Disturbed, and I cringe ever so slightly. I used to love this song but I can't stand it now. I quickly reach over and press the button to skip the song. A wild grin spreads over my face when I hear the opening chords of "I Want it That Way" by the Backstreet Boys.

I whip my head to look at him and he says, "No." I start humming the tune, not giving one fuck that he told me no. "Don't you dare," he warns.

"You areeeeeeeee…" I sing.

"You can stop at any time, nobody likes these guys anymore," he argues.

"My fiiiiiiiiiire…Yes, they do, Cranky Pants, or it wouldn't be on your playlist… The one desiiiiiiiire," I continue to sing. "Believe, when I saaaaay." I take a deep breath to belt out the next part, open my mouth, and—

"I want it thaaaaat waaaay," Collin loudly sings, and it shocks the hell out of me. I blink at him, mute, while he continues to sing. He looks over at me with burning cheeks and a shrug. "Everyone loves them, I blame Andy Samberg."

I'm pretty sure I am going to start catching flies with my open mouth so I quickly shut it. I don't know why him singing to the Backstreet Boys shocks me like it does. Maybe it's because he's so alpha. I shake my head to literally clear my thoughts, and I see him reach over and switch the radio off.

"I developed a bad habit in the military to sing when things got tense to uplift my team—morale, and all that. So now, every time there's a song on the radio or my iPod that I like, I have to sing it. I can't seem to help myself, so unless you want a ten-hour concert featuring me, I suggest we ride without music," he admits, mostly to himself.

Aww, he's embarrassed, if his pink cheeks are any clue, and it makes me want to kiss him. I start to move to do just that when I remember him being an idiot this morning, and telling me we couldn't do this anymore. Ugh, sleep it is, then. Maybe the time will go by faster. I nestle down in the comfortable seats without looking at him, and close my eyes, praying for sleep to find me. Even if it doesn't, I can plot my nefarious revenge on him for stealing my favorite line of the song. Jerky McJerkface.

NINETEEN

COLLIN

WE'RE THREE HOURS INTO THIS TRIP AND ZAYDRA IS sleeping like the dead. She's not moving, and barely breathing, but she keeps talking incoherently to herself. Mumbling is more like it. I could tell when she finally fell asleep, about forty-five minutes ago, because her shoulders relaxed, and her head fell against the seat facing me. It's a good thing I'm driving because all I want to do is stare at her beautiful, sleeping face, and that kind of makes me feel like a stalker. The drive is an easy one that's pretty mindless, with just a light dusting of snow covering the road. I continue to listen to her slight mumbles and breathing with a tiny smile on my face. She's so damn cute.

She suddenly starts jerking and crying out, scaring the shit out of me. I almost swerve into a blue Dodge next to me, and they blare their horn, while giving me the universal "fuck off" symbol. I quickly pull onto the shoulder, and as I put it in park, I hear, "No, Daddy, please! I'll be good, I'll pray tonight. I promise. Please don't! I'm sorry!"

She cries out with her unseeing eyes open, looking around wildly. I grasp her lightly but firmly on her upper arms.

"Zaydra, wake up! You're with me, you're safe. It's Collin," I say evenly. The last thing I want to do is scare her out of a nightmare. "Zaydra, baby, come on, wake up, you're safe. *You are safe.* You're starting to scare me. Nothing is going to hurt you, I'm here."

I continue to soothe her, but my panic is rising every second she doesn't wake. It takes another minute of coaxing but she finally comes out of her nightmare prison. She starts to blink rapidly, and finally, those pretty green eyes clear and she recognizes who has her. I exhale heavily, unaware I had been holding my breath. The pain in her eyes is killing me, and the vulnerability hidden within them. Then, she builds up those walls, shielding herself. She forces a smile up at me from her reclined position.

"Are we there yet?" Zaydra asks, her tone playful, like I didn't just witness her almost break because of a dream. As much as I shouldn't want to, I fucking wish I could be inside her head and learn all her secrets, because she's for damned sure tight-lipped about everything. I should keep my distance from her, but I can't, and it's driving me crazy. There's just something about this girl that makes every sane thought go out of my head.

"You can pretend like this never happened if you want, because you're so desperate to outrun a past that keeps catching up with you at your weakest moments, or you can tell me why you look so terrified. You said, 'No, Daddy, please! I'll be good, I'll pray tonight.' Did your father hurt you, Zaydra?" I grit out forcibly, because the idea of the one person who's meant to protect a little girl the most, hurting her, is abhorrent to me.

"Fuck you, Collin. What did and did not happen to me isn't any of your damn business. Focus on Cammie because you can't save everyone. Stop trying to save me, I was damned a long time ago," she tells me angrily.

Zaydra props her chair back into the upright position, and silently stares out the window. I run my fingers through my hair in frustration. Fine, if she doesn't want to talk, she doesn't have to. I turn away, take a deep breath, and slowly put the vehicle in drive. This drive is already a fuckload of fun. Maybe I can't save everyone, but I can sure as hell still try, though she won't give me a chance. After this morning, I'm not sure I blame her. I need to get my head right anyway because I keep going from wanting to strangle her to wanting to save her. I'm confusing myself.

TWENTY

ZAYDRA

WE DRIVE THE NEXT SEVEN AND A HALF HOURS IN SILENCE. Even during the bathroom and gas breaks, he just grunts at me. I feel guilty but I'm also angry he pushed me like that. He doesn't even know me. Finally, Collin throws it in park and exits the vehicle in front of a slightly rundown house, in the Garden District of New Orleans. He apparently expects me to follow. *I bet he's regretting me coming along now*, I think morosely while I exit the vehicle. He carts the duffle bags up to the house, but pauses and turns to look at me over his shoulder. "Please don't enter the house until I have a moment to go inside and give you the all-clear."

My glacial attitude melts a bit. I love that he's angry but still trying to take care of me. I nod once, and he sets down the heavy bags silently, then enters the house using what looks to be the spare key. He draws a gun from a hidden holster at his shoulder blades—not sure where *that* came from—and is gone for a good five minutes before he reappears at the doorway and motions me inside.

"It's clear. I'd like you to stay in the upstairs room to the right, and I'll take the one next to it, just in case. I know you don't need saving, but I would feel better, and hopefully be able to sleep tonight. We have roughly thirty-six hours until the others get here, and I was hoping we could do some light reconnaissance in the morning before they get here. Are you okay with that?" he asks, with the slightest hint of snark.

Dick. Hot as hell, but a dick, nonetheless. I beam up at him in what I hope is my best beauty queen smile, but it must look slightly deranged by the way his blue eyes widen.

"Of course I'm okay with that, Admiral Assface. That's why I'm here, right? Just don't try creeping into my room tonight because you're lonely. After all, you have Rosy Palmer, and she's the only thing you'll ever need. Please excuse me," I say sweetly, as I squeeze past him to continue up the stairs to my room.

I don't let myself think of how nice it is to not be homeless. I know I'm being a brat but I can't seem to help it with him. He brings out the best and worst of me, all at the same time. He grabs me by the arm when I try to stomp up the stairs—just enough to catch my attention but not enough to hurt me.

"What, Collin? I'm tired, it's been a long drive, and I'm so sick of your hot-and-cold bullshit. So, unless you want to join me for a shower, let me go," I say wearily, and he does. I stare at him a moment longer, with a tinge of sadness. I could very well love this man at some point, but not while his demons, and mine, are between us. I turn on my heel and walk quietly up the stairs. Fuck him and his stupid handsome face. My anger at his inability to be what I want doesn't stop me from putting a sway in my hips, however. I hear his quiet groan as I reach the top and smile to myself triumphantly. Feminine wiles for the win!

I find the room he mentioned. It's not nearly as nice as the one I slept in in his apartment, but it has a bed and that's more than I'm used to. After I take a long, hot shower, I sit on the edge of the mattress and put my head in my hands. I hate when I'm with Collin, I feel whole, but I'm also reminded of how broken I really am. I don't know how to separate the past from the present sometimes. I'm pushing him for more than he can give me, and I'm not even sure I could handle having anything real right now.

But I want real and, more importantly, I want him. I want to be the normal woman in a normal relationship with a man who gives me butterflies. I can see how good it could be in my mind's eye, but it's an unrealistic expectation. I slowly sink back into the pillows, and I can feel silent tears track down my cheeks. I fall asleep, wishing for things to be different, for me to be different. But I'm a pickpocket and he's a millionaire—we're from two completely different worlds.

The next morning, I hear shuffling around downstairs. I can't seem to get my head right when it comes to being here and wanting to be with this man. I yank myself out of my thoughts and get up to start my day of reconnaissance, which makes me feel like I'm in a fucked-up version of a *Mission: Impossible*. You can call me Betty Badass. I make my way down the stairs to see Collin at the Keurig, and I hear bacon sizzling in the pan. The smell of it wafts over to me and I decide I could get used to this sight in front of me. Him, shirtless, in the kitchen, making me breakfast. It's strangely domestic. My stomach decides to growl loudly, and he turns his face to me.

"Sit down, breakfast will be ready momentarily. We have a long day. We're not going near the Warehouse District today, but we are going to do recon on the rest of the city in the immediate vicinity. They know me; we can't afford to look like we're searching for something. So, we're going to play the madly-in-love newlywed tourists. Get a feel for how many people are in this city, and who, if anyone, can give us any more information than we already have."

I make my way over to the breakfast table, and like yesterday, he serves me first, including my coffee that he doctored perfectly. He watches me like a hawk as I take my first sip, and I curse how observant he is. It's too good. He needs to be a dick again so I can resist him. I take my first bite of bacon, and moan loudly with my mouth full, causing his lips to turn up in a smile.

I swear, this is what the euphoria from heroin is like. Collin is way too good at everything, so I glare at him. He just shakes his head and continues to eating. When he's done, he stands and takes our empty plates to the sink. I hadn't even realized I cleaned my plate, but living on the streets, you become used to inhaling your food, so no one steals it from you.

Knowing he wants me to get ready for the day, I turn silently to go change but before I leave, I say, "Thank you for breakfast, Collin," because, after all, my mama did teach me manners, and some polite habits are harder to break than others.

I make my way up the stairs and take out the duffle he brought for me. Inside are all kinds of clothes, from sorority girl chic to gothic chic at a rock show. His thoughtfulness makes my heart skip a beat. I don't know how he had time to get all of this, but I'm infinitely grateful he did. I dress in a hurry, silently laughing at my outrageous outfit that is a mix of sorority with a gothic flare.

Coming down the stairs, I see he's in a pair of jeans and an ice-blue Henley now, with a Saints ball cap on and his Ray Bans to shield his eyes. He could be any other hot man on the street. That's what I loved about New Orleans when I first came here, the anonymity of everyone. Everyone is on vacation and no one cares what you're doing. That's why the crime rate is so high. It goes back to the Mean World Syndrome.

We leave the house hand-in-hand to set the illusion, and decide to walk over to Bourbon Street, the underbelly of this seedy city. It takes about an hour to walk there, but I'm taking mental pictures of everything along the way, like I know he expects me to do. If anyone looks at us too long, mental snapshot, if anyone bumps into us, mental snapshot. As we walk, I check to make sure our items are still there. We are, after all, in the prime place for "borrowers," and most aren't as nice as me.

We finally make it to Bourbon Street, and because it's the middle of winter, it's not nearly as buzzing as it normally would be. We pass so many homeless people, making my heart hurt because, just days ago, I was one of them. Even so, I keep my guard up and my mask of happily-in-lust on. Finally, we stop at one bar, and it's obviously a country bar, with a mechanical bull. I grin mischievously at Collin, who shakes his head very firmly at me, and it's my turn to scowl. He always ruins my fun.

TWENTY-ONE

COLLIN

We're trying to feel out potential informants and she wants to ride the mechanical bull. I don't even know what to do with this girl. I stopped at this bar because I saw two men go inside who looked like the tweaker I met with the note. If anyone has a price for information, it's a tweaker. Zaydra is scowling at the bull like it personally offended her, and I lead her to the bar to order us both a beer. When in Rome, and all that. After paying for our beers—thank God the bartender didn't card Zaydra because she doesn't have any identification—we make our way to a table in the back.

The men are nursing a couple glasses of alcohol, obviously trying to stave off the shakes of withdrawal. Good, they're just about desperate. "Zaydra, I need you to stay here for a moment. I'm going right there to talk to these guys, and I don't want you on their radar at all. Stay back and observe for me. Please?" I murmur quietly.

She looks like she's going to argue for a moment, but surprisingly, she nods. I get up and make my way over to the two guys, pulling out a chair. Dropping into the seat, I shoot them an easy smile.

"Evening, gentlemen. I was just wondering if you had some information I could buy off you," I say, staring them both in their bloodshot eyes. I pull two one-hundred-dollar bills out of my new wallet and place it on the table, out of the line of sight of everyone else in the bar. They look at me, then at the money —they're practically salivating over it.

"What do you wanna know, man?" the leaner one says to me in a scratchy, shaky voice.

"Nothing too big. Just, if you gentlemen have heard any whispers about some bad shit going down around here, maybe involving underage girls." I keep my tone light, hoping like hell I'm not exposing myself to someone who is part of the group, but it's a chance I have to take. The shorter, stockier guy looks at me, his gaze unfocused.

"You a cop?" he sneers at me. I shake my head.

"Nah, man, I promise. I'm just looking for someone. Not looking to bust anybody," I say lightly, and take the last hundred-dollar bill out of my wallet, placing it on top of the other two. I make sure to let them see I have nothing else in my wallet, in case they have any bright ideas, like robbing me. That's the thing about tweakers, they are completely unpredictable.

"Yeah, we heard some things last night when we were trying to score. If we didn't have money for the stuff, and we knew some pretty, younger girls, we just had to bring them along and we'd get enough rock to change our life. We just had to talk to somebody named J." The leaner one sniffs and wipes his nose on the back of his sleeve.

My heart starts to beat fast. Motherfucking J. I know this lead is legit, it has to be. These guys are too far gone to lie. They'd sell out their own mother for a fix right now. I hand him a piece of paper with Ryan's phone number.

"If you all get in touch with J, or hear anything else, call this number. This man may be willing to pay you more based on the information you give him." I rise and walk away, leaving them three hundred dollars richer, and my soul a little darker for fueling their habit.

I reach Zaydra, and jerk my chin towards the door. She stands and takes my hand, giggling lightly, then raises up on her tiptoes and whispers, "They aren't watching. They look like they're arguing on where to go to score. Let's go."

I pull her to the exit. Once outside in the bustle of people, I feel my shoulders start to tense.

"How did you know they had any information? They looked like regular drug addicts to me," she tells me softly. I pull her into an open-air bar and shush her.

"My gut told me they knew something. I always follow my gut. Addicts hear more than anyone ever thinks, but no one is worried because most of the time they can't remember their own name. But when they're jonesing, they'd sell out the pope for a bump," I tell her, then raise my head and look around. I hear laughter coming from beside me, and realize only I could try to pull her to safety and end up in the one gay bar on Bourbon Street.

"This is a nice place, we should definitely hang here for a while, I think. Or, if you like, I saw Hunk O' Paradise over there that I'm pretty sure is a male strip club." There's laughter in her voice, and I'm back to wanting to strangle her again. I look at her with an annoyed expression, which only causes her to laugh more. I grab her hand and race outside.

"You should stop and smell the roses every once in a while, Collin. We just got some pretty great information. They are here, J is here. He's got Cammie still, I can feel it," she whispers softly, for only me to hear, and I feel in my gut she's right. I turn to stare at her, right into her deep green eyes, and I nod once. I believe her.

"Tonight, we're going to go to one of the nightclubs in the city and see if I can score more than drugs from those dealers. Maybe we'll get lucky and they'll have more information than those two," I tell her brusquely. She stares at me for one long minute before nodding, then motions for me to lead the way back to the house. I'm starting to love how much trust she puts in me.

TWENTY-TWO

ZAYDRA

I HAVE THE HIGHEST HEELS I'VE EVER WORN ON—I LOOK like a demented gothic Barbie, with a tight, skimpy black dress, sky-high heels, and enough heavy makeup to make me look ten years older. I almost slammed the door in Collin's face when he handed me this dress earlier. But Collin assures me this is similar to what everyone here will be wearing. He's wearing an expensive suit, with his hair slicked back, and generally not looking like himself.

We step out of the town car he ordered and are ushered inside without even showing our ID's, ahead of the groaning line, as all the people struggle to get a look at this shady businessman and his side-piece illusion we are exuding. I feel like I'm one wrong dance move away from showing everybody the glorious white moon that is my ass. Collin's hand skims over it as we are led to what can only be the VIP area. Not used to this kind of treatment, I'm sure I look incredibly out of place, but Collin is in his element. He whispers something to the sketchy-looking bouncer. I give him a questioning look and he shakes his head slightly. Okay, apparently, I'm playing the empty-headed bimbo tonight.

The waitress immediately comes over to bring us glasses of champagne. "Dom?" Collin questions. The girl nods, staring at Collin like he's the second coming. I shoot her a nasty look. "Go ahead, princess," he tells me, gesturing for me to get a glass first, and she grins at me condescendingly.

"Thanks, Daddy," I say, in my best airhead voice, as I grab a champagne flute. He visibly starts to cringe before he catches himself, and I simply take a sip of the champagne, then lick the excess from my lips, watching as his eyes darken. He snags a champagne flute and sends the besotted waitress on her way, with a fifty-dollar tip and a flick of his wrist. He leans in closer to me and licks the shell of my ear. I shiver and lean into him.

"I've asked the bouncer to hook me up with someone who does party favors. I need them to see that I'm the alpha, so no questioning me tonight. These men are dangerous, and I need the information they might have."

I let out a giggle as I see the bouncer approaching with a man, also dressed in a suit, but the fit is wrong. Something about this man is oily and sinister. Something almost evil. I want to visibly recoil from his presence, and Collin must sense that because he puts his hand on my knee and grips tight, keeping me in place without hurting me or being obvious. I snuggle up to him and start kissing his jawline, playing my part well.

"I hear you two are looking for some party favors? Where are y'all from, I know I ain't seen you two in here before," the man says, in a Cajun accent.

"I'm from Seattle, and I picked this sweet peach up in Portland for a weekend getaway. We're here to party, and when I party, I go hard. It reminds me of college. And I'll use any excuse to get away from the wife. You hear me?" Collin says, matching the oiliness that is this man. We went over our backstory, and while it still skeeves me out, I snicker and continue to kiss his neck as his hand comes down to cup my ass. *It's all part of the illusion*, I keep telling myself, so I don't get turned on.

"Ah, a good family man, wanting to let off some steam. What are you looking for?" the man says after a moment, appearing to accept our story.

"I'm feeling like some uppers for myself, and maybe some X for my lady friend, Mister...?" Collin pauses, trying to learn his name.

"Marcus. I got all that and it can be here momentarily. Anything else?" Marcus says to Collin.

"Not unless you have any more girls that want to worship the ground I walk on, maybe slightly younger?" Collin says with a laugh. I lean back with a pout and mock glare, and Marcus laughs along.

"It looks like you might have your hands full, but if you get bored and wanna trade up, I know a guy," Marcus says smoothly. Collin reaches out to shake Marcus's hand while slipping him a wad of folded bills. Marcus quietly deposits it into his coat pocket and stands. "Party favors will be here momentarily. Pleasure doing business with you." He turns to me. "Hopefully I'll see you later, sweet thang."

I giggle at him and he leaves. I can physically feel my stomach rebelling.

"Not here, Zaydra, not here. I'm sorry. I'm so sorry. I don't like using you like that. I wouldn't if it wasn't necessary, but you heard him. He knows a guy, he knows *them*. They've been in this town trafficking for a decade. It's them, I know it," Collin whispers, and I nod imperceptibly. I thought I left this part of my life behind, but with the return of his demons, my old demons are coming into play too.

The club scene is in full swing when Marcus returns, and I excuse myself to find a restroom. There's only so much of this creep I can take. I breathe deep, then wash my hands and avoid looking at myself in the mirror. I stay in the bathroom for five minutes and finally leave, hoping Marcus is gone.

As I step through the door, I run smack into the devil himself. He grabs my forearms in a punishing grip and backs me against the wall. He leans in and smells me, and I try not to panic. Marcus grins at me and finally says, "I did so want to see you alone. You look like the right type of play thing for me. Your man in there wants younger, I'll take you for myself. You look like you taste sweet."

As he licks my throat, I finally break away, and glare at him.

"Don't touch me, you fucking human pustule," I sneer at him haughtily, playing the spoiled princess I'm supposed to be. "I'll tell Daddy and he doesn't like to share his toys."

I back away and slip into the crowd of people. My heart is pounding and I want to throw up, but I make it back to the VIP section, where I find Collin leaning back on the couch I left him on. I lean down and whisper, "I need to get out of here now. You need to take me home. We need to fight, and make it loud and angry, so we can leave without anyone suspecting anything."

He studies my face for a moment, and I must look dead serious because he pops up off the couch and gets in my face. "You spoiled little bitch. I spent all this money on you, and now you want to leave. What good are you? Your pussy isn't that magical!" Collin yells loudly. I shrink down, but bounce back with bravado.

"You will not talk to me like I'm your wife just because I let you park your shrimp dick inside me. I don't feel good. *I. Want. To. Gooooo,*" I say shrilly. I turn and storm off, fully knowing he's hot on my heels. I hear him curse, then order the bouncer to get us a car.

We finally make it to the exit, he takes me by the arm and whispers, "Zaydra, you better have a good reason for wanting to leave. He was about to get me the guy, I know it."

I jerk away, aware of the prying eyes on us. Playing up my anger, I sneer, "No, I will not suck your dick in the car. Ugh, Amber was right. I should never have come here with you when you can't even make me come."

I then flounce to the waiting car and climb inside, immediately rolling up the partition as Collin climbs in after me. I turn and put my finger to his lips, then hold up the phone I lifted off Marcus. Collin's eyes are incredulous as I explain to him what happened, and I can see the anger seething below the surface.

"I figured, since you were the computer guy, you could hack it and find the information for yourself."

TWENTY-THREE

ZAYDRA

New Orleans stinks. I remember it smelling bad, but this time around feels like it's worse, knowing there's a pedophile ring in this city. Like, you can smell the rot of those men's souls. Now I'm wandering around the Warehouse District, looking like a tourist, thanks to all the New Orleans gear Collin bought me, taking mental pictures as I walk. Collin's men are supposed to meet us at the house he had rented off the Garden District tonight. He's busy hacking Marcus's phone but I need the mental pictures to help. I'm playing the tourist in one of the most dangerous cities in the United States, to find men who hurt girls like who I used to be. It gives me more clarity than I have ever had in my life.

My eyes dart sideways to take in the bustling street, tracking alleyways, every single rundown building I can see. I won't forget any details. I raise my brand-new phone and take pictures of anything and everything, playing up the touristy sorority girl vibe I'm rocking. Wearing no makeup, I know I look young, which was my whole point. My eyes dart over faces to see if maybe I can see if anyone is staring at me, even slightly interested.

Suddenly, I feel a chill go down my spine, like cold fingers tickling down my back. Very inconspicuously, I stop taking selfies with the abandoned warehouses on this block and turn my head enough so I lock eyes with a very tall, good-looking man across the street from me. His eyes are like ice. No humanity, but they're calculating, assessing me. I don't scare easily anymore—life on the streets leeches away the terror at little things—but if this man comes towards me, I might be forced to run. Something about him just gives off the aura of evil.

"Zaydra, you hoebag! I *cannot* believe you left me at that weirdo Airbnb while you did the cool touristy shit yourself! If I find out you went to Marie Laveau's grave without me, I swear I will tit punch you!" Amber squeals, running up to me as quickly as you can in five-inch heels and a leopard dress. What in the what is my sort-of-hooker-friend from St. Louis doing here?

As she shoves some hipster out of the way and smacks her gum at his glower, she reaches me, pulls me into an embrace, and whispers, "Detective Rides-My-Ass brought me along because I've danced for a known trafficker out of New Orleans before. I know some old haunts. And sweet nipple clamps, you seem to have caught the eye of a 'talent recruit.' Collin and Stoney are on the end of the street, Collin said he tracked some dude's phone to a known call log here. They don't want to be made after I gave them a heads-up of whose eye you possibly caught.

"Shit on a stick, sweets, what were you thinking, dressing like this? Not only does it make you look thirteen and boyish, but where'd your boobs go? Did you bind them? Are you *trying* to be bait?" She sounds terrified. As she takes me by the arm, I angle us to get a selfie with him in the background. Maybe he'll buy the sorority girls story. After seeing this man, I have only one concern, and that's to save Collin's niece, Cammie.

Amber leads me away, giggling and whispering for me to join in for us to be believable. This girl, she's smarter than she lets people think. So, we walk fast, giggling with our arms linked, and round the corner. Amber pulls me inside the corner seafood restaurant, where we're seated quickly, out of view of the window. As the waiter takes our drink order and scurries off, I feel a hand bear down on my arm. My hand comes up in a closed fist on instinct, ready to throat punch somebody, when I realize it's Collin in black-framed glasses and a ball cap. I immediately relax. Something about him just puts me automatically at ease. He seats himself next to me while Detective Stone sits down next to Amber. Gone is his suit and in its place are jeans and a gray Henley. He's an attractive man but I just feel no lust or urge to climb up his torso like my favorite jungle gym, like I do with Collin.

"So, what the actual ever-loving fuck were you thinking, putting yourself out there like that? I told you *reconnaissance*. I needed to hack Marcus's phone, and I did. J was in his call log, and we tracked it to this street when we spotted you. I literally just wanted you to take a look around. I meant walk up and down the street maybe twice—your memory would take care of the rest. What the fuck, Zaydra?!" Collin says, clearly frustrated.

I feel my ire rising. Where does he get off? I open my mouth to respond when the waiter returns with the drinks. I smile politely at him while the guys order drinks. I return to my full attention to Collin as soon as he leaves.

"I'm literally doing what you asked of me. Recon, nothing more nothing less. Did I put myself out there slightly as bait? Yes. I'm from the streets, I know how to get noticed by men like this. I'm on their radar now, if I wasn't last night. What better way to get closer to getting Cammie than to have someone inside?" I tell him with a fierceness I wasn't sure I had.

He's still clutching my arm across the white-clothed table, staring at me angrily, like I had done something to jeopardize the mission he brought me on. I hated it. I was doing this for him, and for the younger me no one fought for.

"She got his attention, Collin, that's for sure. He could be a key player. He could even be J. He wanted both of the girls, you could tell. He followed her, making phone calls, before she even noticed him. Then, when Amber showed up, he made three more calls," Ryan says quietly to Collin. For once, Ryan is on my side. That, or he totally wouldn't mind me being kidnapped.

"I don't have to like that she almost got herself kidnapped by her own stupidity. She shouldn't tempt fate. She could have compromised everything," Collin snaps.

"Excuse me, please, I need to use the restroom," I choke out. I rise, with Amber on my heels. *I will not cry. I will not cry.* His opinion of me doesn't matter that much. I hurry to the back of the restaurant where the bathroom is located. I'm having a hard time holding back the tears, but I do through sheer will. Finally, Amber and I enter the bathroom and close the door.

"CAPTAIN WEIRDO DOESN'T MEAN you're stupid, candytits. He was obviously just feeling helpless, and when alpha men feel helpless, they lash out. What you did was unintentionally stupid, but smart at the same time. You're a fearless bitch, aren't you?" Amber exclaims. She's looking at me like I'm a badass, I'm so not. I have a lot of fear in me, but I can outrun anything, even fear. I splash water on my face with shaking hands to calm myself down.

Amber continues while I get a hold of my emotions, "He's sexy as sin though, isn't he? I bet you climbed him like a bunk bed, didn't you? Whew, sexual tension. I wouldn't mind licking him like a lollipop. He certainly seems like more fun than Detective Stonewall Me Jackson. He's about as much fun as grabbing an electric fence. Let me tell you though, I feel like they both have big dick energy."

As soon as she says that, I choke on my own spit and start hacking up a lung. She kindly pounds me on the back. "I figured that's a yes. It's okay, details aren't necessary. Appreciated, but not necessary."

I'm still shaking my head as I exit the restroom, coming face-to-face with Collin.

"I'm just gonna give you two lovebirds a minute to kiss and make up," Amber says, squeezing past me, and she bolts. Traitor. I watch her cross the restaurant and sit at the table with Ryan. She puts her hand right in his lap, and I can't help but laugh when he quickly slaps it away. I can see her pout from here. My laughter dies when I see the look on Collin's face. It's a mixture of disappointment and anger. I mentally steel myself for a "daddy lecture," but what comes out of his mouth surprises me enough that the glare slips off my face.

"I was wrong to call what you did stupid. I didn't mean to infer that you were stupid. You took a risk last night for me. That was uncalled for, and I'm sorry, Zaydra," he tells me quietly. I feel my eyes fill with tears. Why does this man make me so emotional I lose my head? "I care about you, more than I should, and the thought of you getting taken, like Cammie did, makes me lose it. My temper is barely controlled, and I wanted to kill that man with my bare hands for looking at you like his next meal ticket, even if he might be our first lead to Cammie. I would have killed him if he tried to grab you." His hand comes up to caress my face, and the pad of his finger runs across my bottom lip.

"I wasn't actively trying to put myself in danger. We had no idea if they would be out and about today, we just have a note saying the Warehouse District was their last known location. So, I figured it couldn't hurt to try to make myself up as bait. I've been through worse, Collin."

He growls at me—actually growls—before his mouth roughly slams down on mine. I've never been angrily kissed before, and let me tell you, my lady bits are perking up like a dog about to go for a walk. I kiss him back just as hard, using all the passion inside of me, when a throat clearing interrupts our embrace. He raises his head slowly and glares at the manager of the restaurant before grabbing me by the hand and leading me back to our seats. I'm still dazed by that earth-shattering kiss when I see Amber fanning herself with a plastic child's bib that has *Got Crabs?* printed on it. *Bitch*, I think, smiling to myself even as my cheeks flame.

"Now that you two have deigned to join us, can we please order and eat, so we can get out of here before Blondie molests me anymore?" Ryan grumbles. Amber just gives him a similar deranged beauty queen smile, like I have.

"So, was that a nightstick in your pocket or were you happy to see me, Stoney?" Amber sweetly replies, as she bats her eyelashes at Ryan and blows him a kiss. Her eyes meet mine and she mouths, "Big dick energy."

"Lord help us all," Collin says wearily. Yep, that about sums it up.

TWENTY-FOUR

COLLIN

IT WAS DUSK BEFORE THE REST OF RYAN'S TEAM SHOWED up, and much to my surprise, all of them are from my old Special Forces unit I haven't seen in years. These men are my brothers, and they are thankfully rallying behind me when I need them the most. There are eight of us in total, not including Thelma and Louise.

Amber has been quietly gossiping to Zaydra every time a member of my old unit walks into the house. If I didn't know any better, I would say they're rating them as they come in the small house, like we were at a gymnastics meet. I thought men were bad—we have nothing on these two. Kaysen, my FST guy back in the military, comes up to me first right when he stalks inside. At six-five and three hundred pounds of pure muscle, this man is someone I'm completely glad is in my corner.

"Lieutenant. I'm sorry to be here under these circumstances, but I'm really fucking glad to see that ugly mug of yours," he says as he grips my forearm in a warrior greeting. "I can't believe these miserable fucks took your niece. Do they have any idea who they're fucking with?"

"Kavanaugh, man, it's good to see you. I'm so glad you're

fucking here, we have so much to—" I start to say when I'm interrupted.

"*Holy crib midgets*! Zaydra, he's a ten, look at him! That blond hair, and those muscles…hey, come on, don't shush me, he looks like Thor. Come to Mama, Thor!" Amber shouts across the makeshift war room we have set up in the living room.

I see Zaydra turning bright red, shaking her head at Amber while trying to shush her. Ryan casually strolls across the room and plops down, then whispers something in Amber's ear. Her mouth drops open and she turns her head and hisses, "Bite me, Detective, you know nothing about me." She turns to Zaydra and says, "Switch with me before I shank Mr. Wants to get Murdered over here."

I shake my head at the girls and at Ryan as the whole room grows silent.

"May I introduce Zaydra Miller and Amber James to you gentlemen. Ladies, this is Kaysen Kavanaugh," I say, gesturing to the mountain next to me, who is shaking his head with an amused look on his face. I point at the first man who came in. "This is Jensen Michaels, our resident explosives expert."

Jensen, being shy around females, even though we've been told he's the best-looking out of our ragtag group of misfits, ducks his head and tips his chin at the ladies, ignoring Amber's three-fingered wave, as I continue with the introductions. "Anderson Russo is the guy you want to seek out for field operations planning and execution."

The Italian man sprawled in the arm chair across from the ladies grins wildly at them and copies Amber's three-fingered wave in Zaydra's direction. I clear my throat, which has tightened with jealousy, and steam ahead. "Miguel Martinez is our weapons extraordinaire," I mention, as the tall Latino man tips his imaginary hat at them and blows me a kiss. Shaking my head, I point at the last two men leaning against the wall leading into the kitchen. "The pretty boy twins are Shane and Malcolm Gibson. Shane is our medical expert and Malcolm is our tech guy. Both are also our best marksmen, don't ask which is better."

The twins are silent but manage a nod to the girls, which was honestly more than I expected of the Angels of Death. A lovely nickname they were given, and that's what they were known as around the village where we served the last tour overseas.

"*Hello*, man candy. Wait, if it's more than one attractive man, are they known as men candy, or man candies? Oh well, I digress. I'm Amber, I'm a prostitute-in-training, but I'm a stripper extraordinaire. Oh! And I'm super bendy. I think that's all I got for sharing time," Amber says, triggering shocked looks on the faces of nearly everyone in attendance. She blows a kiss to Ryan, who just mutters something about bullshit.

"Well, following that, I'm Zaydra. I'm a certified 'borrower' of things, and I have an eidetic memory, which is why I'm here. Also, I think I'm bait," Zaydra states, matter-of-factly. She talks with her hands—fuck, she's cute.

It's taking everything in me to stay where I'm standing, and not pick her up and throw her over my shoulder to take her out of the room, so none of my dirty fucking friends can look at her and fantasize, like I know they're doing. Fuckers, I know they're looking at those plump lips and juicy fucking tits, which her tank top barely contains. Bait, my ass—she's temptation, pure and simple. I must make a strangled noise in my throat, because all heads whip around to me. I clear my throat again and shrug my shoulders sheepishly.

"Wait…borrower of things. Are you trying to say you're a thief?" Kaysen says to Zaydra. "Which unlucky bastard did you steal from, Sergeant Stone or the Lieutenant?"

She looks him dead in the eye and says, "Your lieutenant and I just had a friendly misunderstanding about his wallet. He's so absentminded, losing his wallet and then blaming me. I mean, really, he's lucky I forgave him for his accusation and agreed to come on this trip. He's also lucky I'm such a kind and intelligent person to be able to look past his Neanderthal tendencies."

She punctuates her statement by picking at her fingernails like she's bored. Her sarcasm and slight arrogance make my dick go to half-mast, but pretty much everything about this girl makes my dick hard. Even when she's insulting me. "Plus, he knows I could kick his ass," she finishes and sniffs primly.

Kaysen starts to guffaw, causing laughter to erupt from nearly all the inhabitants in the house. Even the twins smile. Zaydra shows a hint of one, and glances up through her lashes at me, before she quickly looks away.

"All right, you heathens, down to the situation at hand. We know that Cammie was last seen in an abandoned building in the Warehouse District," Ryan says in a hard voice. "These men have a vendetta against Collin, and they've had her for way too fucking long. It's not like last time where we got our orders from the TOC, this is personal. This is on us, not the government. Collin's niece is tough, but these sick bastards aren't known for their hospitality. Collin, man, I'm not saying this to hurt you, but we've been through this situation before, with the senator's daughter. She could be addicted to drugs, she could have severe Stockholm Syndrome, or she could be dead. We don't know. We do have confirmation they are still working out of New Orleans, under the leadership of someone named J."

A muscle ticks in my jaw as I sit down on the arm of the couch, next to Zaydra. "She's not dead, Ryan. These psychos get off on torture and money, not killing the girls. If they wanted to ransom her, they could have. Fuck, if they wanted to kill her, they would have done it already, and I'd have found her body. I believe this is personal, so these sick fucks are keeping her alive and she's going through who knows what kind of hell. But they made sure someone knew she was alive, so it would get back to me. I have a gut feeling this is a trap for me," I grit out to my men.

"I don't expect any of you to go in with me. There's a potential chance for massive loss of life. I will subject no one to that." I meet all of their eyes, one by one, ending with Zaydra, whose eyes I lock on the longest. "That being said, I sincerely hope you'll come into hell with me, because I don't think I can get Cammie back without you all. I'd fight the devil himself for my niece, but I would sell my soul before I got any of you killed."

"With all due respect, Lieutenant, fuck you for thinking there was even a doubt of us going into hell with you. We're brothers—well, and sisters now, but to whatever end, we have your back," Jensen says quietly, while the rest of the men nod solemnly at me.

I know my smile shows terrifying emotion behind it. "Good. All right, listen up, dickskins, here's the plan..."

TWENTY-FIVE

ZAYDRA

Wait, he wants to plan, *NOW*? That isn't a very good idea. I mean, I know my brain is pretty much mush after meeting the supermodel group that used to be Collin's unit. Seriously, so many tens in one place, I'm surprised myself or Amber hasn't spontaneously combusted yet. But to plan before we've even located the group doesn't sound very smart.

"It's called being preemptive, Zaydra. We are just planning on finding them, not planning on how to get Cammie back when we don't know where to start looking yet," Collin says, obviously exasperated with me. Holy shit on cracker, I must have been thinking aloud.

I inwardly cringe at my lack of a filter. I haven't been in "polite company" for a long time, or literally anyone's company besides my own, even if Collin *did* call everyone a dickskin. He's staring at me, waiting for my next outburst, I'm sure, so I simply give him the "please, continue" wave.

He lets out a grunt of frustration with me. "We think we've made slight contact with a scout for the ring. At this point, it seems like it's more of a trafficking ring than just a pedophile ring. It doesn't seem like these wastes of space discriminate based on age. Whatever makes them money seems to be the motivator, because today, Zaydra made herself to look young, and Amber looked twenty-one, easy, and the man was salivating over the idea of them both."

Ryan jumps in, "We have a gut feeling he was contacting his handlers about them. He will surely be there tomorrow, looking for them. And I know that doesn't seem likely in a city as big as New Orleans is, but they hooked him, I know they did. So, I say we use them as bait, but we don't let them get taken. Just allow him to be enticed enough to slip up, so we can follow him back to the epicenter."

"Why don't we just plant GPS trackers on the girls and allow them to get taken? It would be faster, and bait only works if someone *takes* it," Miguel states nonchalantly.

"No!" Ryan and Collin simultaneously yell. Amber and I look at each other. She shrugs as if to say, *male posturing, what are you going to do?* I roll my eyes slightly.

"I know you don't think Amber and I can take care of ourselves, and I can't speak for Amber, but I've taken nearly every type of defense class there is. From Krav Maga to Jiu Jitsu, I know how to handle myself. Honestly, Collin, I would do anything to help your niece," I announce, staring at the man in question, wondering how I'm going to stop myself from falling in love with him. His jaw is ticking and he seems angry, but I'm literally just trying to help. I lift my chin obstinately.

"Zaydra, you're here purely to help with reconnaissance and planning. I can't put an untrained civilian in the middle of a dangerous trafficking ring, let alone, two. Especially since we don't have one hundred percent proof that Cammie is there," Collin growls at me, and leans close enough to try to intimidate me, but Amber reaches over me with her pointer finger, puts it on his forehead, and pushes him back until he's upright on the couch arm. This girl is fearless—Collin can be terrifying when he wants to be.

"She's offering to help because it's the *right thing to do*, you butt nugget. Yes, this girl's brain is important to this mission, I get that, but none of us would be here unless this was important. You want your niece back, I don't fault you for that, but if your best bet of finding her is through Zaydra and I? You should utilize your assets. The first thing you learn as a stripper is how to profile men. Which ones are going to tip the most, which ones are going to be grabby, which ones are dangerous, and which ones just wanna talk. We both can bring something to this mission, bait or not," Amber says intensely.

I know my mouth is ajar because this is the first time I've heard her really talk, intelligent and sincere. By the way Ryan's eyes are flashing, he recognizes that little tidbit too. Collin clears his throat.

"Zaydra, you were bait last night, and it didn't sit right. Let's just try this my way. For once, can we just agree that maybe my planning could be right? We have intel, thanks to you. You don't need to be kidnapped so we can find her. We're so close."

TWENTY-SIX

ZAYDRA

AFTER SEVERAL HOURS OF GRUELING INSTRUCTION AND questions, I finally climb the stairs to go to bed. Amber has her own room at the other end of the hall across from Collin's room, and my room is adjacent to his, unfortunately. I know he's all tortured and brooding, but I'm still angry he shut us down before giving us a chance. I know he has a lot going on, but when I was in his arms, I felt safe. It felt right.

I push open my bedroom door with a sigh, and throw myself down on the cool sheets, pulling the blanket over my head. I close my eyes and truly appreciate the feeling of warmth and fullness. Homelessness, I have a feeling, is a memory that never leaves you. It makes you truly appreciate the little things, like a blanket, new clothes, running water, or being full. A tear leaks from my right eye onto the pillow for the life I could have had if my family had been normal.

I sit up with a start when I hear a knock on the door, and I realize I must have fallen asleep because I have drool on my face. I wipe my face quickly.

"Come in." Collin steps in to the room and my heart jumps into my throat as my lady bits perk up. "Hi," I say, after we both stand there for a moment, saying nothing. I mentally face palm myself. *Hi* is what my brain comes up with? Scintillating.

"Hi, you hurried out of the living room earlier, before I got your attention. I wanted to tell you I'm sorry I keep sticking my foot in my mouth when it comes to you. I do appreciate all the help you're giving me. You could never know how much it means to me," Collin says, rubbing his hand on the back of his neck, like he's nervous.

Humanity is weird, society is even weirder. I mean, we've both seen each other naked but we can't have a serious, in-depth conversation without being nervous. I find myself staring in to those deep blue eyes, wanting his arms around me more than my next breath. Wanting to open up to him. Wanting him to really see *me*, not the poor girl, or the brokenness inside I disguise as strength.

"I know you're worried about me, but I'll be fine. I want to help you. I need to help Cammie. I won't be a hindrance to this mission, I promise."

He searches my eyes for what seems like an eternity, and holy smokes, when did he get so close to the bed? He leans down and kisses me softly on the lips, and I can feel them tingle from the contact.

He whispers, "I know. I don't know much about you, Zaydra, but I know that you're loyal, and you have an incessant need to save others, and you attract misfits. The question is: when are you going to stop being so strong and let someone else take care of you?"

And with that question, he turns on his heel and leaves the tiny space that makes up this room. As the door closes, I let out an exhale, wondering when my life got this complicated. Dredging up old memories is never a good idea for me, but why do I feel like it may be the only way to get this man to stop running from me. I'd have to stop running from the past.

I heave a giant sigh and flop myself back on the pillows, still fully dressed, because some habits die hard. I stare at the ceiling, pondering the idea of a life with Collin. As absurd as it is, the thought of the millionaire and the thief who stole from him, in love, makes me drift off into a peaceful sleep with a smile on my face.

TWENTY-SEVEN

COLLIN

"COLLIN! COME ON, HONEY. PLEASE, WAKE UP! YOU'RE scaring me!" Zaydra screams.

I become aware of myself; I'm in my bed, with Zaydra pinned underneath me and my forearm against her throat. I spring away from her, and wipe my hand down my sweaty face. Confused, I sit back on my haunches, while she catches her breath. Our eyes are locked and I can see concern and fear in her gaze. I realize I must have been having a nightmare—a pretty bad one, if the twisted sheets and my drenched T-shirt are any indication.

"You were calling out and groaning, and you sounded like you were in pain. You helped me through my last episode, I just wanted to be here to offer you comfort. I didn't know you'd think I was a threat. I'm sorry I startled you," she states, sounding upset.

I hang my head a bit in shame. I would never put my hands on a woman, but the nightmare was so real, I had no control over myself. "Do you want to tell me about it?" she asks soothingly as she scrambles down to sit next to me, placing her hand on my shoulder.

I jerk away from her touch, still emotionally unstable from

the nightmare. "Like you did with me? Oh wait, you fucking didn't. I'm alive, not hurt, you can go."

I know she doesn't deserve my ire, but her hot-and-cold shit is driving me crazy. Zaydra rears back at my words, as if I slapped her. She stands abruptly and glares down at me, but the light from the street catches her eyes and I can see the sheen of tears, which makes me feel like a right prick. I start to apologize, but before I can get a word out, she waves my words away, laughs airily, and starts towards the door. Before she makes it, she stops and turns back to me, and sticks her tongue out.

"I've had a hard life, Collin. I don't mean to say you've had it easy, and I get that you're afraid for your niece, but imagine what she's going through. Now think about this: What if her captor was her father, that abused her and then sold her to a trafficking ring disguised as a religious group? Family is supposed to protect you, love you. Mine did not. So, fuck you for making me dredge up these memories.

"You want me to share? Fine. I was eleven when my mother died. Damn near broke me, but I was twelve the first time my father raped me. Yes, the *first* time. It was my place as the woman of the house, he said, but I was thirteen when he decided to share me with the other preachers in the district. I was fourteen when he sold me because he said I had demons in me. My animosity towards him, and my memory, made him feel like I had the devil inside me. Even though he 'sold' me, he was still in charge. He would check in with my 'owner' and see my progress. He said if I was good, he would buy me back. I didn't escape until I was seventeen.

"*Years*, Collin. I was raped and abused and degraded for years. My father still searches for me; he's almost caught me a couple of times. Cammie has been in there months, and the thought of that is horrifying, but we will get her back, and she can recover from it. I did. As much as I possibly could. Now you know that I'm broken, and my demons have been brought to light. I'm done with you tonight. Don't ask for things that I know most people can't handle," Zaydra says, baring her soul to me.

As she talks, my heart breaks a little more for the child she never got to be, as my rage towards a man I don't know grows. I'm so lost in my own musings after her revelation I don't notice she left at first, closing the door quietly behind her.

I'm so blindsided by her confession I don't immediately go after her. My thoughts are racing, thinking about everything she went through. What I subjected her to last night, pretending to be my play thing. Letting me grope her, letting Marcus think she was a commodity to trade, and I find myself roaring, "*Fuck*!"

I put my fist through the wall next to the bed. It does nothing to soothe the helpless rage inside. I grab my phone from the nightstand, and call my friend, Mitchell.

"Mitchell," he barks.

"Carson, it's Reeves. I need a favor, man. I need you to find someone for me," I grit out through my anger.

"Reeves, good to hear from you, man. I didn't think I'd hear from you again after all those dead-ends with Cammie," he says amicably.

"Nah, man, we got a lead on Cammie. I know you did your best with her, and I know you have a vast reach. I need you to find someone for me. I don't have his name, but I have the daughter's name. Zaydra Miller, approximately twenty-four years old, born in the south, most likely Alabama or Florida. I need you to find her father. This is top priority. I will pay whatever, as long as you get back to me fast." I speak quickly, anxious to follow Zaydra.

"Do I want to know why this man needs to be found urgently? Never mind, don't tell me. Consider it done. Wire the first part of my fee into my account in the morning. Give me a couple of days, I'll find out the last time he took a shit, the last person he smiled at, or the amount of sleep he got last night," he states confidently.

"Just find him for me," I growl into the phone a second

before I disconnect the call. I toss it on my bed and stride out of the room. A minute later, I'm in front of her door, jerking it open. The first thing I see is her huddled form under the blankets, the mattress shaking with her quiet sobs. Right then and there, I'm certain I would sell my soul to take the pain and memories from this woman. I know I'm in love with her strength, humor, fierceness, and her tendency to borrow things that aren't hers. Fuck, I'm in love with her, regardless of the fact that I just met her a few days ago. Her soul is crying out for mine, I feel her in my bones. She's the other half of my heart, I just know it. I don't care that she stole from me. She could take everything I owned and I'd let her do it with a smile on my face.

TWENTY-EIGHT

ZAYDRA

BARING ALL OF YOUR UGLY SCARS TO SOMEONE YOU CARE about is like being naked in front of a million attractive people. The vulnerability of it makes me sick to my stomach. Opening the vault where my memories are stored, because I have to compartmentalize all of them or I'll go crazy, is like opening a floodgate. Memories of my past are flashing behind my eyes. Of my mom kissing my scraped knee. Of my father throwing me up in the air and catching me while I squealed with delight. My mom in her hospital bed, each breath getting fainter as does the sound of beeping, while I beg her to stay with me, as I beg her to fight the cancer harder. Of my father, just staring down at her limp body as she passed, and then turning and walking out without me. Of the first time I woke up in the middle of the night to him slipping into my bedroom, smelling of alcohol. Of me trying to get away from him and him yanking me back by my hair.

A thousand other memories assault me as I whimper and cry silently, to not wake anyone else in the house. I can feel myself start to fracture into pieces, when I smell him. Collin's scent wafts to me first, smelling of cedar and freshness with a slight hint of sandalwood. It smells safe. I feel the bed dip and then his arms are pulling me into the shelter of his broad chest.

He rubs my shoulders lightly as I continue to silently cry, remaining stoic and making noncommittal noises to soothe me. His presence is like glue that keeps me from shattering completely. "I'm here, I've got you," is what he keeps murmuring to me.

Any other man, I'm not comfortable even shaking hands with. But this man fills me with a passion I've never known, and brings me a peace I've never even conceived. I snuggle further into his chest. As my tears dry, I find myself with wandering hands, wanting to erase the bad memories and replacing them with good ones. Thankfully, he got rid of his sweat-drenched shirt. I start to explore every dip and indentation of his eight-pack abs and his defined chest. I pull lightly on his chest hair and he grunts slightly, but makes no move to stop my perusal. I move my right hand lower until it encounters the waistband of his gray sweatpants, and run my finger lightly over the ridged waistband, pleased when I hear a light groan from Collin. His skin is burning hot as I trace the tips of my fingers back and forth over the skin right above his waistband. And, hello dick print. I love gray sweatpants.

I smile triumphantly into his chest, then start pressing kisses to his right pec muscle as I slip my hand into his sweatpants, and find him without underwear. I grasp his cock firmly and he groans louder into my hair. I can barely fit my hand around his cock. I start to stroke him from root to tip; the satiny skin is hot and pulsing as I continue to tease him. His breathing starts to change, and I push myself down to his waist. The only need I have in this moment is to worship his cock like he ate my pussy that first night.

"You don't have to do this," Collin says huskily, staring into my eyes. In response, I pull his sweatpants down his lean hips to his muscled thighs that flex under my hands, and his dick springs free. The Glorious Monster is really what its name should be. I lick my lips and look back up into Collin's eyes.

"I want this, I want you. You can be my lollipop for the moment." I grin salaciously before I engulf the head of his cock. This time, the groan he unleashes is loud enough to wake the dead, and if I wasn't so busy with his cock in my mouth, I would have laughed. I hum my appreciation instead, and I hear his whispered, "Oh fuck."

That just makes me want to suck the soul out of his man through his dick. I want to make him remember me, even if he can never be completely mine. I want this. My hand drifts down between my legs to play with my clit as my head bobs down until the head of his cock hits the back of my throat. I breathe in through my nose, relax my throat, and deep throat the shit out of him. His hips buck, and he starts fucking my face with a helpless abandon. Just as I'm about to come with my own ministrations and because of the hot-as-fuck animalistic noises he's making, he rips me away from his cock. I make a sound of protest that is drowned out when he slams his mouth on mine in a punishing kiss.

His hand creeps in between my legs, and he finds the flood of wetness that leaks from my pussy. "Good fucking girl, getting nice and wet for this cock. You want it bad, don't you? You want me to stretch that pussy out, huh? Pound this little pussy until you scream my name. Come so hard that everyone in this house will be jealous of me for years to come. You want everyone to hear what a dirty bitch you are, don't you?" Collin growls in my ear huskily.

"Please," I whimper.

"Please what, baby? What do you want?" he says, teasing.

"Please fuck me, Collin. Please make me come. I need to come so bad," I pant out, feeling like I'm coming out of my skin. My belly tightens with my impending orgasm as he lightly runs his first two fingers up and down my slit, without making contact with my clit. Teasing me so bad, until I feel like I'm about to go insane.

"Filthy girl, where do you want me to fuck you? You want me to fuck you with my fingers or my cock. Come on, filthy girl, tell me what you need," he says, his tone mocking, and I know I've pushed him to this sexual breaking point, wanting me to feel him for years to come, like I had wanted him to remember me.

"God, please fuck me wherever you want with whatever you want. Please, Collin, just give me what I need," I choke out. He leans down and bites my nipple, as he thrusts two fingers into me, and rubs my clit with the other hand. I'm so close, I start begging incoherently, slightly closing my legs. He uses his body to keep my legs spread, and he curls the two fingers inside me upwards, hitting my g-spot and sending me off like a bomb.

I start to squirt, which has never happened before, and he removes his fingers and spanks my clit, extending the orgasm to one of the longest I've ever experienced. I swear I see God. I must black out a bit, and when I finally come aware, he's got my face in his hands. With the sweetest kiss to my lips, he slips his massive cock inside me, making my eyes roll back.

If you've ever heard of tantric sex, that's what it felt like. Little mini orgasms going off with every thrust of his cock in my pussy. "There's my good fucking girl, squeezing my cock with that tight pussy. Milking me, hungry for my cum. You feel so fucking good, so fucking tight. Like nirvana."

His words cause a new flood of wetness in my pussy, which has him groaning as he continues to pump into me, hard and fast. His movements grow jerky and his rhythm becomes rougher, more erratic. He starts to rub my sensitive clit and I cry out his name as I come again. He shoves into me one more time, and exclaims, "Oh fuck, Zaydra. Dear God."

My mouth curls into a smile as I rub his sweaty back. I guess he saw God too.

TWENTY-NINE

ZAYDRA

I COME AWAKE SLOWLY, FEELING A HEAVILY MUSCLED ARM thrown over my waist, which causes me to smile. What a good feeling. I thought I would feel emotionally raw and ready to bolt after baring myself to Collin last night, but I don't. I feel closer to him than I thought was possible. I turn my head to see his brown hair flopped over one eye, his face slack with sleep. He looks beautiful, like the statue of Adonis, just pure masculine beauty. I'm completely lucky to even be in this man's bed for a moment in time. I gently slip out from under his arm and pad to the bathroom with a change of clothes. As soon as I finish dressing, I catch the scent of coffee and bacon, and my tummy grumbles. Shooting one last look at the Greek god in my bed, I sigh and walk out of the room.

I make my way down the stairs, and it looks like the men are all awake. Their sleeping bags are all empty, so I make my way to the kitchen, and I'm greeted by the sight of seven shirtless, incredibly well-built men. I'm momentarily stupefied as they all stop to stare at me. I give a slight wave, like a dumbass, but any female would be awkward if confronted with this much hotness.

"It should be against the laws of nature to have this much man candy in one group." I hear from behind me, and I turn to see Amber standing with a cup of coffee in a pink silk nightie. She smiles at me and winks. "I heard y'all cleaning your pipes last night. If you want to let me watch next time, I'd be happy to conduct, or film. You know, for science," she states, then winks and blows me a kiss.

"I wouldn't want you to get jealous of my tits again, or of my skills either. I make men see God," I state smugly, and she just laughs and breezes past me into the kitchen, where all the men are standing, jaws dropped at our conversation. Miguel's mouth is open and pieces of his bagel start to fall out. Anderson quietly leans over and shuts his mouth with one hand, shaking his head as he mumbles something about crazy females.

I make my way to the Keurig and pop in a K-cup. I breathe in the scent of fresh brewed coffee, a luxury I haven't been able to afford in a long, long time. As soon as I take the first sip, I groan in my bliss. I hear throats clearing behind me, and whirl around to see Collin standing there, glaring at all the men. Their eyes are all on the floor, except Ryan's—his are glued to Amber in her silk nightie, who is steadily ignoring him by studying the God-awful flowered wallpaper. Interesting.

Collin makes his way over to me, and I move out of the way of the Keurig, thinking that's what he's going for, when his arm slips around my waist and he kisses me soundly in front of everyone. It lasts long enough to make my pussy clench. When he finally breaks our connection, I'm panting with my cheeks flaming as he turns to make himself a coffee.

Amber looks me straight in the eye. "That shit is foreplay, and unless one of the man candies wants to volunteer to clean my pipes, I'm going to need you to take pity on my cobweb-filled vagina and ease up on the hot-as-fuck PDA," she says haughtily and mock glares at me.

At that, it's Ryan's turn to glare all the other men into submission. Fucking alpha males. I mentally roll my eyes; to Amber, I just blow her a kiss. She catches the air kiss with her hand and puts it to her vagina, and then she winks at me again. I decide right here that this girl is my best friend. Baby prostitute or not.

I clear my throat and offer a weak smile to everyone as I slip from Collin's grasp, and head towards the kitchen table to sit with Amber. "Bitch," I mutter to her with an exaggerated glare.

"Hoebag," she responds with a wink. I find myself smiling over the rim of my coffee cup. Collin pulls out the chair next to me, gracefully sits, and shoots me a look as if to ask if I'm okay. I give him a barely perceptible nod, and smirk at him as well. I'm enjoying this moment. If I try hard enough, it's almost like we're just a regular couple having breakfast with friends…and a bunch of hot, shirtless dudes. But reality is setting in fast—Collin's niece is still a prisoner of the worst kind. She needs to be found, and fast.

I take a deep breath. "I've been thinking I could go back to the Warehouse District today, possibly make contact with the procurer. See if he takes the bait, because at least then, we can really know if Cammie is in New Orleans, assuming they have the girls grouped together, which is usually the case. If she's not there, you come in and get me, no harm, no foul—and you'd have men to question." It's so silent you could hear a pin drop. I look up at Collin from underneath my lashes, and, huh, that's a fun shade of red. He's leaning in and shaking his head adamantly.

"Fuck no. Are you kidding? After everything you told me last night, you think there would be any way in hell I would let you be bait? I'd much rather send Ryan in there in a dress and hope for the best," he snarls at me.

"Thanks dude," Ryan interjects.

"Even if your niece's life is at stake, Collin? She is absolutely the number-one priority here. No one looked out for me; we need to look out for her. By any means necessary, she's what you need to focus on. I can take care of myself. Please," I plead with him.

"No, I won't put you in danger! This isn't your fight, this is mine. She is *my* priority, and I cannot get her out of this situation if I'm worried about you!" he yells at me.

With narrowed eyes, I stand from my chair and stalk out of the room. I know he's trying to protect me, but after years on my own, this kind of hovering leaves me feeling a little stifled. I stand next to the window in the living room, trying to cool my temper and calm my fast-beating heart. I feel the hot pinprick of tears behind my eyes, and blink rapidly to will them away. I have the weirdest habit of crying when I'm angry. It's a helpless anger, because I know I shouldn't be upset with him nor he with me, but now emotions are involved, and the situation itself is volatile enough. I feel the realization that I'm being a brat tickle the back of my mind, so I swipe the tears away with one hand, at the same time I feel a presence behind me.

"I keep making you angry, and raising my voice. I am sorry, I don't mean it. This whole situation is fucked. But I won't apologize for taking your safety seriously. You are a civilian, you are not trained. Not in the way myself and these men are. You will not be bait, you will not put yourself in harm's way. You are here for one purpose—you have the unique ability to remember things exactly from just a snapshot in your mind. I need your help with planning and strategy, not for the actual rescue mission. That's why there are seven other highly trained men in there. They've done extractions like this before.

"We need a plan and we need to find her location. We have possibilities right now, but I need to focus, and fighting with you is not helping Cammie right now. Please don't ask me to let another woman I care about get kidnapped because of me. Please," Collin rumbles from behind me.

My shoulders droop a little. I know he's got a lot of points, but it's hard to accept I would be a hindrance when I have this burning feeling I need to be there.

"I get it. I don't like it, but I get it. You have to promise me one thing, though," I say with conviction, whirling around to look him straight in the eyes. "Promise me when you go to do the rescue, you'll be equipped with a body camera for me to see everything you see. I need to be there in some way. Your comm guy, Kaysen, or Malcolm, can do that for me, right?" I know we haven't even found her yet but I know in my gut, we will. I'm still searching Collin's eyes, when he gives me a sharp affirmative nod, and I let out the breath I didn't realize I was holding. I smile at him encouragingly and pat his chest. "See, big man, it wasn't that hard to compromise, was it? No snarling needed."

He captures my hand and kisses my fingertips. "Zaydra, nothing with you seems to be easy, including compromise. Let's go back in there and try strategizing again without going head to head, okay?" he says with a wink.

"Did you say head?" I grin evilly and lick my lips.

"That comes later, and so will you," he replies and smacks me on the ass. The saucy bastard. I shake my head, grinning, and walk ahead of him into the kitchen. Ryan is by the kitchen window, speaking low into his phone while the other men are talking in hushed tones at the kitchen island, and Amber is at the kitchen table, staring at us. She smiles innocently at me, and I don't trust it. She doesn't pull off the angelic look well.

"Guys, look, Mom and Dad made up!" she quips. Jensen blushes, and she says, "Really All-American, that's what makes you blush? We need to get you to a strip club ASAP. Come into Dark Angels with me when I get back to St. Louis, and I'll introduce you to some of my really nice friends."

"What, you're not trying to sell him your wares, Ms. James?" Ryan butts in, after hanging up from his call.

She throws him a glare. "Oh no, Stoney baby, I would eat him alive." She turns back to Jensen and licks her lips, tilting her head to the right. I'm honestly impressed she did it without the hint of a smile. Especially when I see the cherry tomato that is now Jensen's face, and the fact he's now choking on air, and hacking to get his breath back.

"Ry, what was the call?" Collin breaks in.

"I got a tip, from the tweakers you gave my number to.

There's a recently abandoned building on the edge of the Warehouse District, where some incredibly unsavory characters—meaning the people who told them about the girl-for-drug trade—have been seen entering and leaving at all hours. My guy at the local P.D. said sometimes girls were spotted, but very few and far between. It could be what we're looking for," Ryan tells us.

"Or it could be a regular crack house. This *is* New Orleans, after all," Kaysen replies.

"But it does pair with the tip I got back in St. Louis. Her last whereabouts were the Warehouse District. At the very least, it's worth looking into," Collin muses. "Zaydra and I will go take a look at this building and the surroundings. It will be a quick look, but I think it'll be effective with some tech to show us heat signatures, which I'm assuming you have?" He directs his attention to Kaysen, who nods affirmatively. Collin nods back and looks at me. "You up for another field trip?"

"I thought you'd never ask," I say. He's obviously trying to make up for excluding me earlier. I think I would do anything this man asked of me, including walking down Bourbon Street in a flamenco outfit. Not that that would be out of place here.

THIRTY

COLLIN

THE ABANDONED BUILDING IS RUNDOWN AND EXACTLY what you would expect for the edge of the Warehouse District— crumbling, with massive graffiti on every inch. From our vantage point in my Range Rover, the outside looks like it could very well be the home for a crack house, or a wealth of homeless people.

Using the heat signature vision goggles, I can see at least twenty people, possibly more. Most of the signatures are much smaller, so I make the assumption a large portion of the inhabitants are female. I don't want to get my hopes up. It can't be this easy. My niece could be yards away, and I have to resist the urge to go in there with my Beretta and put a hole in all the males. I tamp down the rage, rip the goggles off, and look over to Zaydra, who is studying the entire place with binoculars, taking in every detail. Good thing for tinted windows.

"There's a window on the third floor that I haven't seen a single shadow in. It doesn't look like anyone is walking by, or even in that room," Zaydra states.

I raise the goggles again to look where she's pointing, and she's right, there are no heat signatures. Every other room has some inhabitants, but not this one. It also has a hole in the glass.

This could be our point of entry if we go in through the roof. It could be the surprise advantage we need.

"Wait…Collin?" Zaydra asks, her voice shaky, and I turn my head to her. "What does your niece look like?"

I quickly pull out my phone and scroll to the photo my sister Collette had distributed when Cammie first went missing. I hold it out, and hear her breath catch.

"What? What is it?" I exclaim, because she's scaring me.

"I just saw her. In the second-floor window. It was a flash of her face, but I know I saw her. That hair and those eyes, it's her," she says, shocking me. The words are like lightning in my blood. I have to save my niece. It's my only thought. I reach for the door handle, and am pulled back by a dainty hand on my right arm.

"You can't storm in there right now. We're severely outnumbered, not to mention, outgunned. She's there, that's the confirmation we needed. Let's get back to the house and plan your next move. You cannot leave this vehicle. The tinting might be hiding our identity right now, but the moment you leave, they recognize you. We become open targets and Cammie is the one with the bullseye on her back. *Let's go!*" she tells me, forcefully tugging my arm to pull me away from the handle.

I exhale sharply and nod. I put the Range Rover in drive and take one last look, silently promising Cammie I'll be back. That I'm coming, and she won't be in hell any longer after tonight. I need to keep my head clear; I need to save my niece. She deserves that. I don't need to get all of us killed by being hot-headed. I look over at Zaydra, and I can see her mind racing a mile a minute. She found her for me.

"Thank you for seeing her. Thank you for giving me more hope than I didn't know I had. Thank you for recognizing her, even when you had never seen her before. Strategy and rescue are next. She's getting out. All those girls are getting out," I assure her, with more confidence than I've had in a long time.

"Of course she's getting out. She will be okay, I know she

still has hope. They won't have broken her yet, especially with you as her uncle. She'll know that you'll move heaven and earth to find her."

Zaydra words are comforting as she places her hand on my knee. I give her a small smile and focus on getting us back in one piece. I feel shaky. I've never lost my cool amidst a mission before, but the mission has never been family before. She saved my ass.

"Fuck, I wish I could get her now. Every minute she's in there makes me want to kill her captors even more." I speak my thoughts softly, watching the road. Zaydra's hand tightens on my knee, then she sighs.

"We'll get her. A few more hours, Collin, and she'll be free. Trust your men, trust yourself, and trust me. We would all walk through hell to spare this little girl any more pain. She's getting out tonight. She's alive, that is what matters." Her words soothe the beast inside me rattling its cage.

"But what if it's like last time. What if they shoot her, and she just allows it, like a lamb to slaughter? My sister would never forgive me, I would never forgive myself," I say, hating to voice the painful thoughts that are burning my brain.

"That won't happen. Do not allow that thought to take hold because it will just create doubt. I have every confidence in you, and your team's ability to get Cammie out in one piece. It's too important for any other outcome. Focus on getting her free. There is no other outcome," Zaydra says firmly.

I flick my gaze to meet hers, and the assurance I see there has me taking a deep breath. I let it out and slowly nod.

Tonight. She's getting out tonight.

THIRTY-ONE

ZAYDRA

THE MEN ARE CIRCLED AROUND THE COFFEE TABLE, WITH building plans that weren't here when we left. Anderson apparently bribed someone in the city clerk's office for building blueprints, and now we have a better idea of what they are walking into. Collin is speaking rapidly, telling them about all we saw and the weak spots we found. I add details he leaves out, that my memory dredges up, of sewage pipes and back alleys. The men are looking from him to me and nodding quickly. They are no-nonsense. They were everything I wanted to rescue me when I was young. While it never came for me, it will for Cammie. I'm glad she has this. She's going to need it.

"Why would she be near a window?" Amber asks. "Don't these men know you're looking for her? Something feels off here."

"The ease of finding her *is* a little suspect, Lieutenant," Shane rumbles.

"Suspect or not, she's getting out tonight. She's in hell, guys. I can't leave her there." Collin's voice breaks on the last word and my heart aches for him.

"It might be a trap for Collin, but they're not expecting all of us. They can't be. Three of us will enter from the roof, like planned. Two will enter from the ground floor in front, and two will enter from the ground floor around back. All exits covered. No escape, she's coming home tonight," Ryan states firmly for all the men, who acknowledge his words with a sharp nod.

I see why he's Collin's number two. Seeing these men plan, smoothly strategizing, is something of beauty. It's seamless how well they work together. They might be out of the military but you'd never be able to tell. Miguel gets to his feet and goes out to the black SUV he brought and returns with vests, bulletproof ones.

"Kavanaugh, rig these with cameras for the girls. The Lieutenant told us they're to be linked in remotely from here, in case they pick up something we miss. Malcolm already has our comm links secured. We need video up and streaming," Miguel says, tossing the vests to Kaysen, who snatches the vests one by one. He cracks his knuckles, looks at Collin, and salutes him.

"Aye, aye, Captain…err, Lieutenant," Kaysen replies in mock hilarity.

The men are a flurry of activity, preparing for the night ahead. Something is niggling at my brain, something that is bothering me, but I can't seem to think of it. Amber, sensing I needed an activity to keep me busy, comes over and sits on the couch next to me. She sits very quietly for a moment, just sharing the space, completely at peace in the silence.

"Do you love him?" Amber whispers to me after a while. I turn to give her a completely bewildered look. "Don't give me that look, sweets. You know what tall drink of water I'm talking about."

"I don't know. We only met a few days ago, when I stole from him," I whisper back indignantly, feeling defensive because I'm not used to explaining myself to people. I've been out of polite society for a long time. She looks me straight in the eyes.

"So, you haven't admitted it to yourself yet. That's fine,

booboo. He's a fine piece of man candy, though. Lucky bitch," she muses, more to herself than to me, with a dreamy look on her face. "I bet sex with him is like riding every ride at Six Flags at once, hashtag big dick energy."

I can't help but start giggling like a school girl because I've never actually heard anyone use hashtag in a sentence before. I can't even argue with her, so I just smile with my cheeks heating.

"Are you a psychic? That's exactly how I would describe it. He's so patient but dirty at the same time." I find myself gossiping like an old lady at a hair salon, but we're interrupted when Collin walks over, and I feel my face flame hotter. He gives me a long look, and Amber elbows me. I glance over and she's doing the hashtag motion and mouthing big dick energy, which makes my face flame more. What is my life right now? Collin squats to where we're eye level.

"You okay?" I nod, not trusting myself to speak. "I know it's not easy, not being a part of the actual mission, but I'll need you to be my eyes here. Malcolm is getting the laptop set up with surveillance body cam feeds. You'll see what I see and what the rest of us see. I need you and Amber to warn us if we miss something. We're leaving a radio here with you as well. I trust you, and I need you to trust me to carry out this mission," he finishes in the same soft tone.

"I understand. We're here to enhance the mission and rescue Cammie, not put everyone else in danger. Cammie is number-one priority. Just bring her back, get her out of that hell. Do that for her, but do it for me as well?" I tell him.

"I promise," he says solemnly.

"'Come back with your shield, or on it,'" Amber leans in and whispers, and we both turn to stare at her, confused. She shrugs. "I saw it on *300* and I thought it was badass, and y'all were having a moment right in front of me, so I felt left out." She then blows Collin a kiss, who just shakes his head. He straightens for a moment, then bends at the waist and takes my mouth in a scorching kiss. It goes on and on, when I feel a hand rubbing my back. I break the kiss and see Amber rubbing me and Collin's backs as she blinks innocently at us. "Threesome?"

Collin bursts out laughing, as do I, and he's still shaking his head as he walks to the door. He starts barking orders for the men to get loaded up. They are a flurry of motion because it's finally getting dark outside. It's showtime, apparently. Kaysen makes his way to us with the laptop, which has multiple dark screens on it.

"It's all set up, we just need to turn the cams on our vests on. Once that happens, you'll get the video. With this"—he holds up a radio—"Malcolm rigged it so you'll hear the audio. If you press the button on the right and left at the same time, you can communicate with us. You ladies understand?" We both nod. "Give me your words, ladies. If I don't have verbal confirmation, the Lieutenant will skin me alive."

"I understand," I tell him, then I look to Amber, who is gazing at Kaysen in that man-eater way of hers.

"Yes, sir, daddy, sir," she says saucily. Kaysen just shakes his head and walks away, muttering about crazy females trying to get him killed. After a moment, I understand why, as I see Ryan lounging on the stairs, glaring over at us. Amber must see him too because she curses under her breath.

Pulling a script from her book, I lean over and whisper, "Do you love him?" I wink conspiratorially at her.

"Like having a particularly painful case of syphilis," she whispers back sweetly. Someone is in major lust and major denial, all at the same time. So, I just let it go, because I'm nice like that. Amber raises her voice at Ryan when he just continues to stand there. "Safety in numbers, Detective. Run along, make sure Collin comes back to my girl here." She bats her eyelashes. He looks at her for a long moment, salutes, and follows the other men out the door. Amber then lets out a long breath. She turns to me and smiles in her crazy way. "The men are gone, is this where we make out?"

I choke on my own spit. "I... I... I'm not a lesbian," I stutter out at her. She smiles deviously, and I see her holding the radio, with the buttons pressed. I hear a chorus of male groans and she laughs. This girl is going to be the death of us all. I stick my tongue out at her, which only makes her laugh harder.

THIRTY-TWO

COLLIN

MY HAND TIGHTENS ON THE STEERING WHEEL UNTIL MY knuckles are white. I've never been this fucking scared before a mission. I have too many thoughts racing through my head. What if Cammie is like the senator's daughter? What if they have her so addicted to drugs she's damaged for life? What if she's damaged for life anyway? A hand comes down on my shoulder and my brain halts its dark ramblings. I turn my head slightly and meet Ryan's eyes, nodding at him to let him know without words I'm okay. I have to be, I'm Cammie's only hope at this point. I trust these men with my life, so I'm willing to trust them with hers as well.

We ride three quarters of the way to the warehouse, but park in an alley far enough away, in as secluded an area as possible, so they won't see us coming. It's now the dead of night. All of us are wearing black mission pants and shirts, and we start to pile out of the SUV as Kaysen and Miguel start to hand everyone their vests. I strap mine on and Malcolm heads over to me. "Lieutenant, permission to touch your bod to turn on that cam for your girl?"

Smartass. I nod an affirmative to him. He twists it and taps, and I glare at him, knowing I could have done it myself, but he's trying to get my mind off the dangerous, volatile situation we're about to head into.

The men are all finishing up with their vests and turning their cams on, when we hear, "Breaker, breaker one-nine, we are confirmed on the cam show. Who is getting naked this time around? Please tell me it's going to be Thor?!" Amber's voice says over the radio. It is too loud in the silent evening, so we automatically switch over to the earpieces and turn the handheld off.

"Amber, we are not truckers, you don't have to use that dialogue. And for the love of God, just put Zaydra on the radio, so Kaysen doesn't get murdered by Ryan, okay?" I find myself gritting out. I think my friend might like this psychopath. She's funny but psycho. Ryan is glaring at me and Kaysen, who is looking everywhere but at him.

"Desert Eagle, this is Pickpocket, do you read me?" Zaydra's voice says over the radio. I roll my eyes; apparently, the girls want to have nicknames. I'm apparently in love with a psycho too.

"Yes, Pickpocket, we hear you. We need you to watch silently so we can complete this mission accurately, unless you see something important. Clear?" I growl at her. We can't afford distractions at this point. We are too close to the goal at hand.

"Clear," she says again over the comm link we share. The men are finishing their prep and weapons are being strapped to each of the men in turn. I turn to arm myself with knives first, followed by handguns, and then my AK. I'm thanking God Miguel wasn't stopped on his way to New Orleans with his trunk full of all of our weapons. Gun charges for ex-military are not high on the agenda, and him carrying over state lines could have been bad, even if they all are registered.

Once we're all outfitted with weapons, the feeling of leadership comes back to me. The emotions start to leave my body as I go back to being the no-nonsense commander. I signal all eyes to me. "Every one of us has an important part to play tonight. Shane, Ryan, and I go in through the roof to the third floor.

Russo and Kavanaugh will go in through ground floor front, Jensen and Miguel will go in ground floor rear, and Malcolm, I need you posted up on the building on the right side, for a bird's eye visual. We're going to get one shot at this, guys. The girls are watching, if we miss anything, but my niece is top priority. Secure her and get the other girls out. Understood?" I say quietly. I get a chorus of affirmatives and we break up into our respective infiltration groups. This could go a million ways, but I'm praying tonight, it will go the right way for once.

Shane and I move in sync up the street, staying away from the lit areas. Reminding me of all of the missions we went on before, this area is mostly deserted and half of the street lights don't work, which is perfect for a trafficking ring. I'm not a superstitious man but I feel the evil in this place. Shane must too because he crosses himself even though he's not Catholic. He whispers, "Just in case."

We continue our slow descent into the madness that is an abandoned part of New Orleans, silent and deadly, like we were trained. We are finally a stone's throw away from the building, ready for our climb, and I hear warning bells go off in my head. We get our climbing rope from the rucksack that I'm carrying and the bells grow to a scream.

"Lieutenant, there's no heat signatures inside," Malcolm says in hushed whispers, confirming my gut reaction.

"Not possible, we scoped them out not six hours ago. They were here," I intone softly, in disbelief more than anything else.

"Lieutenant, whoever was here earlier, they're not here now. There's no one inside. No one alive," Malcolm says again over the comm link, barely above a whisper. I let out an inhuman roar, and race in through the front of the building with Shane, Ryan, Kaysen, and Anderson hot on my heels.

I see...nothing. The building is completely empty; not even a piece of furniture is left. I see something glint and catch my eye in the middle of the first floor. I race over to see my money clip I gave to Marcus last night, with a folded note attached. Before I can open the note, Kaysen's voice rings out.

"Guys, why haven't we heard anything from the girls? Not a peep. I know you said not to say anything, Lieutenant, but I figured once they heard there was no one inside, we'd hear something?" He says this and my blood runs cold. I quickly open the note.

"'You think we weren't waiting for you to make your move? Now we have your lovely girl *and* your Camisole. How much money they'll fetch. What beauties they are. You'll never see them again. J,'" I read in a voice thick with emotion. "*Goddammit, no! Fuck!*"

I should have seen this coming.

"He said he was watching you, and he got Zaydra, but what the fuck did they do with Amber?" Ryan roars, and we all take off towards the car in a flurry of motion. The rest of the men meet us there, and I say a prayer this note isn't true, that this sick fuck is simply playing with me.

THIRTY-THREE

ZAYDRA

AMBER AND I ARE TAKING TURNS LISTENING TO THE GUY'S live feeds of them in the car. We can hear the silence they are riding in, occasionally throwing out something in military lingo about FST's and maps, and honestly, it's boring as hell. After our little CB radio talk and the cameras going live, we're supposed to be quiet and observe. My nerves are shot from worrying for them, and for Cammie. I need them to get into the warehouse already. I get up from my seat on the couch, needing to do something. Amber glances up at me from her turn at the monitor.

"Where are you going, sweets?" she calls to me.

"I'm just going to get a glass of water. I don't know, I need to do something with my hands because my anxiety is getting the best. I just wish I could be there, you know? I feel like I need to be doing something more than staring at a computer screen," I yell back at her from the kitchen. I pour myself a glass of water and think better of it, so I pour two glasses—one for me, and one for her—so she can't bitch I left her out. Smiling to myself, I return to the living room to find Amber with a knife to her throat, and the man from the Warehouse District with ice-colored eyes is staring straight at me.

"Hello, baby. I'm so glad you could join us. The crazy bitch here isn't the one I'm looking for." He pauses, with his hand over Amber's mouth. "Unless you're both taking his dick, then maybe I *do* need both of you."

He grins at me and licks down Amber's cheek, and I can hear her muffled screams from my vantage point by the kitchen door. I could probably make it to the back door and away before he caught me, but that would mean leaving Amber to fend for herself. He and I both know I would never do that. I come into the room cautiously, my eyes never leaving the knife he has to her throat. When I get too close, he lets the blade bite into her neck. A trickle of blood slides down her neck, and I can hear her pained whimper, so I quickly back up.

"Go sit on the couch, baby, Amber and I are quite cozy like this. Tell me where the boys are. Go on, be a good girl and tell me," he croons, his deadly beauty looking more inhumane by the second. I'm struggling to hold back tears, feeling so angry and helpless.

"They're finishing arming up and walking to go into the warehouse," I choke out, wishing like hell I could warn them as I come to sit on the couch in front of the computer monitor.

"And what do you think they are going to find in there, Zay?" he says to me with a low laugh. He punctuates his statement by removing his hand from Amber's mouth and kissing her hard. I let out a strangled cry and Amber screams at me.

"Run, Zaydra! Just run—" She's cut off when he digs the knife deeper into her throat. He's looking at her like she's crazy but then he shoots me an evil grin and I know if I do run, he'll kill her. He chuckles low in his throat and whispers something in her ear. I see her go completely white, begging me with her gaze to go, but I shake my head at her sadly. I'm not willing to take the risk. She means too much to me to even try.

"Well, Zaydra, what do you think they're going to find there?" he asks again, like he's losing patience.

"Tell me you didn't kill her. Tell me the sick fucks you work for didn't kill Cammie. I'm the only one taking Collin's dick. Please, just let Amber go, she has nothing to do with this. I promise." I feel tears slide silently down my face, unable to imagine the horror that's awaiting Collin in that warehouse. "How did you know they were coming?" I can't help but ask.

"They will find nothing when they get into that warehouse, sweet Zaydra, baby, not even a trace that anyone was ever there. That will drive him fucking crazy; that, and the knowledge I have his precious fuck toy. You didn't think I didn't have people watching him every second of every day, baby, because I don't work for any-motherfucking-body. My name is J, and I'm going to be worse than those little nightmares that you keep having," he says coldly, and I feel the chill of his words skitter down my spine.

He just keeps staring down at me while holding Amber, then leans down and whispers something else to Amber. The scream that breaks free from her will haunt me for the rest of my life. He spins her around and slashes her across the chest, and I see bright ruby-red blood spray. I scream with everything in me as I pop up from the couch and run headlong at him, fully intending to take him down with all my body weight, but he feints left, and I feel a hard blow to my head. As I fall to my knees and everything starts to fade to black, my last memory is of staring at the pool of blood growing around Amber's motionless body and the sound of cold laughter in my ear.

I COME AWAKE SLOWLY to a pounding in my head. I can't see anything but I feel movement that's making me nauseous. The back of my head feels wet and matted, like I was bleeding, and I'm dizzy. It feels like I'm in a fast-moving vehicle, and that thought alone is terrifying. It took them six months to find anything about Cammie, and they wanted Collin to find them this time. They won't want him to find them again unless he's going to kill me, and Cammie. I start to rustle against my restraints, tugging and pulling as quietly as I can. They feel solid, like—

"They chained you to the truck," I hear a sweet voice say. "There's no use in struggling. If it looks like you're trying to escape, they'll just make you wish that you hadn't tried." The voice sounds young, like she's a teen!

"Cammie, sweetheart, is that you?" My voice is only slightly muffled through the mask they have over my head. "If that's you, I'm friends with your uncle, and I know it doesn't seem like it right now, but this is a rescue mission," I tell her soothingly.

"I don't know you. Uncle Collin would never send a civilian in after me, and you don't look military—you're not much bigger than me. If this is a rescue mission, consider me under-whelmed," she says with teenage snark I choose to ignore, because hello, bigger picture. She confirmed she's Cammie, and she is, in fact, alive.

I give a mental fist pump and I'm so happy for a moment, before I remember the clusterfuck of the situation we're currently in. My one job besides reconnaissance was to *not* get myself kidnapped, and I went and did just that. I gotta say, when I volunteered for this before, I don't think I thought it through. Everything hurts, and I think I might be sick. This shit is for the birds.

"Well, it's good to see that you still have a sunny disposition, and honestly, you're right, this wasn't exactly the plan. But I can guarantee that they are hot on our trail. They'll find us," I muffle out again, trying to get her to trust me. I'm fairly certain they'll be coming for us, or at least, they could be.

"Ma'am, no offense, but after six months of these people, I don't know if anybody is coming anymore. They chained me up here and dragged you in. They usually put me with the other girls, but now they put me only with you. I don't think that's a good sign. Don't talk to me like I'm a kid. I don't think anyone in here is a kid anymore, even the eight-year-olds," she says, sounding so lost, and my heart breaks when I hear how young some of them are. My helpless anger threatens to overwhelm me. None of these kids should be here and the world shouldn't have sick, depraved people that sell kids for money. None of this is fair. The truck slows to a stop.

"He's coming," Cammie whispers, and I hear the fear in her voice. I know who put it there, I just don't know why. Why is J so obsessed with Collin, and therefore, Cammie and I?

I hear the doors to the compartment we are in swing open and then, "Hello, ladies, did you miss me?" Cammie doesn't answer and neither do I as I try to control my breath, praying he thinks I'm still unconscious. "Aww, beauties, I have this lovely truck recorded and bugged, I know you're awake. Don't wanna talk to me, angel?"

I hear a slap and a whimper from Cammie. I yell out a ragged cry of anguish and throw myself against my bonds. The cuffs bite deep into my wrists and there is no give at all. "There she is. Mama bear is coming to play with me, Camisole, isn't that fun?"

J laughs and I feel him come closer. I'm not sure how I know, but I feel his presence hone in on me. I will him closer to keep him away from Cammie.

"What do you want, you sick fuck?" I scream at him. He just laughs at my pain and starts to stroke his hand up and down my stomach. He stops at my breast, cupping it, and I jerk back from his touch as much as I can.

"Ah, ah, none of that. Ask Cammie, it's better for you if you go along, because my patience only stretches so far. I'm going to enjoy tasting you," he leans in to whisper to my bagged head.

"Boss! They reached the house, we gotta keep moving!" I hear a voice scream out, one that sounds entirely too familiar.

"Fuck! Fine, Marcus, you whiny fuck, let's go," he yells back, turning and whispering to me, "We will pick this up later, pet, and you better not fight or I'll pick it up with Cammie and make you watch."

He places a soft kiss on top of the bag, and I almost lose the contents of my stomach right there. Wait! My breath catches when I realize they've reached the house. They knew I was gone —Amber probably told them. Fuck, Amber! Oh God, she can't be dead. I pray harder than I have in my life that Amber's alive. That girl has too much fire to die; she would spit on the Grim Reaper if she could.

"I told you it would be worse if they knew you were trying to escape. It looks like it's going to be worse on me and not you," Cammie tells me softly, and I hear a sob slip out at the desolation in her voice.

"I promise you, Cammie, I don't know how yet, but I'm getting you out of here. I promise, okay? If you have lost all hope and only believe in one thing, believe in that," I choke out through my tears, as I hear her lose her battle and give in to the sobs. I just hope I'm not lying to both of us.

THIRTY-FOUR

COLLIN

WE DRIFT INTO THE PARKING LOT OF THE HOUSE IN THE Garden District, and Ryan and I are out of the truck like bolts of lightning. He makes it into the house first and I head upstairs, thinking they would be there. I hear Ryan's cry from the living room and haul ass down the stairs to see Ryan holding a bleeding Amber. There's shattered glass on the floor, but no Zaydra. I sink to my knees as the other men shoulder their way past. Amber is so still, but Shane checks her pulse. After a moment, I register he's screaming at me.

"Lieutenant, she's got a pulse. It's faint and thready, but there *is* a pulse! Fucking Collin, snap out of it! I need an ambulance STAT!" He snatches her from Ryan and puts pressure on the wound to staunch the bleeding. As I hear Jensen call 911, Amber opens her eyes and locks onto me.

"I put the GPS tracker on her that Miguel gave me." Her voice is barely above a whisper. "He took her, I tried to get her to run. I'm sorry, Stoney," she finishes, then loses consciousness.

"*Goddammit, Amber, wake up!*" Ryan yells. He moves to try and get her to wake, but Shane cuts him off, shaking his head. Her breathing is labored but audible. She's out, and anyone else in her situation, with her wounds, might already be dead, but she's hanging on like a hair on a biscuit.

"She's out, Sergeant, but she's still alive. This girl is fighting like hell. We need that ambulance *now!*" he yells to Jensen after addressing Ryan.

"ETA, two minutes out. Everyone but Shane needs to go. If Amber put a tracker on her, we can't be too far behind them. We need to go now. We still have our mission," Jensen says, with more authority than I have ever heard him use, which is good because he's witnessing his two commanding officers fall apart.

He's right, though. I shake off the numbness and Kaysen moves towards me with the computer, looking at me with hope in his eyes. I glance over at Amber, lying there so still, knowing she felt the mission was wrong before it was a go. She told us so, then went behind our backs and got with Miguel for a tracker, in case anything happened.

"The tracker is working. It's putting her on I-10, going towards Baton Rouge," Kaysen tells me, and I look over at Ryan. He nods at me, and we both rise to our feet. Warriors about to go to war for the people we love. We all file out to the SUV and this time, Kaysen jumps in the driver's seat. He glances over at Ryan. "She's gonna be okay, man. Shane wouldn't let her not be. She seems like she'd fight the devil himself to live for one more day."

Ryan is eerily silent. He just nods his acceptance to Kaysen's words and doesn't say a single thing to anyone.

"Miguel! When the fuck did she get a tracker from you?" I bark at my friend. He cringes at me, looking both chagrinned and fucking happy he went around my direct order not to involve the girls. We're damn lucky he did right now, but it doesn't make it any easier.

"She cornered me during lunch today, when you and Zaydra went to talk after you had gotten back. Amber felt something was wrong and she wanted two trackers, just in case something went to hell tonight," Miguel says, not apologetic in the slightest.

"Two trackers? Where the fuck is the other one?" I ask angrily, knowing she didn't put one on herself.

"It's in here with us; she put one on you when you and Zaydra were kissing. She distracted you with the 'threesome' comment. She didn't want there to be a chance that either of you would lose the other or not know what happened. Like, with your niece. Amber is perceptive as hell. She felt something was off, and tried to help. Despite people thinking the worst of her, she's a romantic at heart," Ryan tells us all.

It shocks me into silence. I didn't feel her put a tracker on me. What is it with me and these women, that I don't notice when they pickpocket me or put a tracker on me?

"Tits, man, it's always the tits," Malcolm says from his quiet area in the back of the SUV, letting me know I said the last question out loud. I hear a few chuckles, but most of us stay silent for a good thirty minutes until we hear a low buzzing from a phone. Ryan pulls out his phone and reads the screen before taking a deep breath and quietly depositing it back in his pants pocket. We're all waiting with bated breath to hear what he has to say.

"Shane and the EMTs kept her alive until they got to the hospital. She crashed once on the way there, but they brought her back. She's in surgery now. She's lost a lot of blood, but so far, she's alive. Shane is going to send me updates as he gets them. He told them he's her fiancé since I'm pretty sure she has no family," Ryan tells us quietly.

We all let out a sigh of relief. She's still alive, she's fighting. That is all we can ask for right now. Kaysen's phone pings and I tense; he sent the tracker signal to his phone.

"They have about an hour head start on us, but it looks like they stopped moving right outside Baton Rouge. We'll see if we can use this window, however long it is, to catch up to them," Kaysen tells us confidently.

I feel my spark of hope spread into a wildfire. She is a wildcat and she escaped one trafficking ring before, she can do it again. She knows how to fight, I've seen her in action, and if she gets a chance to run, she's faster than almost any man I have ever seen. They better hope that wherever Zaydra is, she's bound tightly, because if she gets free, she'll rain holy hell down on anyone she perceives to have wronged her, or Cammie. Fuck… Cammie. Tears prick my eyes. My niece wasn't at the warehouse, I don't know if she's alive or dead. I just know I fucked up on my mission. They knew I was coming, and I put two ladies I care about, that I love, in danger. If anything happens to either of them, if I never find them. I will never forgive myself.

"Drive fucking faster, Kaysen, this isn't *Driving Miss Daisy*. Ryan, call the state troopers and let them know we are in pursuit of a trafficking ring with a new kidnapping victim, and that we are coordinating with the Feds to take them down, but we are hauling ass and can't afford to be stopped. Get an alert on the description of Zaydra out as well as Cammie; if anyone sees either of them, they are to call the troopers, who are then to call you. Understand?" I bark to everyone.

Feeling the authority in my voice, Ryan gets on the phone and Kaysen's foot hits the floor on the gas pedal. The SUV leaps forwards and we are well on our way to getting to Zaydra.

THIRTY-FIVE

ZAYDRA

THE GENTLE SWAYING OF THIS TRUCK IS DOING NOTHING for my head injury. It is only causing the nausea to build. I might also have a concussion, and while it isn't good to self-diagnose, I'm considering myself Web MD up in this bitch. I have had plenty of concussions and this seems like a doozy. I feel the bumps start to sway me to sleep. So, I keep jerking myself awake, which causes blinding pain to shoot through my head.

"Cammie, sweetheart, I need you to talk to me, keep me awake. I have a concussion and I'm almost going to sleep. I need you to keep me talking. Can you do that?" I say, asking for the teenager's help, knowing I need some sort of distraction.

"Okay, I don't know what to say though," Cammie says, and for the first time, she sounds her age, and terrified. I'm hit with the wrongness of the situation again.

"Tell me what happened to you, sweetie. How did you get taken?" I ask, still trying to discern why these people are so fixated on Collin. I hear Cammie sniffling lightly. "Oh, sweetheart, you don't have to tell me if it's going to make you cry. I'm sorry."

"No, no, it's fine. He said your name is Zaydra, that's a pretty name. I'm gonna call you Auntie Z, I hope that's okay. I got in a fight with my mom a couple months ago. She wouldn't tell me who my dad was, even though everyone at school knew their dad's names, at least. I begged her and begged her; she just wouldn't tell me. She didn't even give me a reason why, just that she would tell me when I was older. I told her I hated her, Auntie Z. The last thing I said to my mom was I hated her."

She begins to cry but fighting her way through the tears, Cammie continues her story. "I was meeting my friend, Charity, at the mall. We were going to get a smoothie and watch for boys. There were always some cute ones from my school that would be there. I took a bus to the mall and I didn't even make it inside. I was walking towards the entrance and then I felt a pain in my head, and then everything went black. I woke up on a dirty bed, and the guy that was in here, he…he…he..." Cammie cuts off on a sob.

"Cammie, baby, it's okay, you don't have to say this part. I know, sweetheart, I've been where you are. Your mama still loves you, she hasn't stopped searching for you, and neither has your Uncle Collin. They both love you to pieces. I was fourteen when I was sold into a trafficking ring, just a little older than you are now. They used to do horrible things to me, and make me do horrible things, but I know that it wasn't my fault, like it wasn't your fault. You didn't ask for any of this to happen to you and neither did I. We're going to get through this, Cammie, because you and I are survivors, and we have one thing this time that I didn't have last time," I say to her, wishing I could see her face and hug her.

"What's that, Auntie Z?" she asks softly.

"Your Uncle Collin," I whisper back. She's completely silent after that. The silence stretches so long, I think she must have passed out, and the only thing I have to keep me awake at this point is the faint sound of traffic outside the truck we're stored in. It's getting harder and harder to fight the headache I have and to keep my eyes open. Finally, I just let them drift closed. A five-minute nap never hurt anybody; it's not like I have places to be, at this point. I snort quietly to myself, which shoots pain through my head. Yeah, a five-minute nap sounds like a good plan right now.

I jerk awake after what feels like years later, disoriented and still unable to see. The loud clang that woke me up sounds again. I realize the men are hitting the outside of the truck, trying to scare us, and it takes everything in me not to shout obscenities at them. A blast of air hits my clothed body, letting me know they opened the door to the outside of the truck. I lightly jerk my chain, frustrated I can't currently escape.

"I told you I'd get to have fun with you, didn't I, sweetheart? You don't look as pretty as you did at the club, but the bag over the head isn't called for. You're not a butterface," Marcus says to me, snickering at his own joke as he gets closer. "Boss man says I get to have the pleasure of stripping you two ladies of your clothes. 'Cuz you won't need clothes where you're going."

He snickers again like he's fucking Kevin Hart, and if the bag wasn't on my head, I would roll my eyes so hard. I sit up straighter when I hear Cammie whimper, and the sounds of tearing cloth make it to my ears. I strain even more against my cuffs, letting the metal tear the delicate skin of my wrists enough to where I feel a warm trickle of blood.

"Get your fucking hands off her," I growl towards the sounds, angry I can't see what's being done, and even angrier I can't prevent it.

"Tsk, tsk, wait your turn. I've never been into little girls. You're more my type, sweetheart, don't worry," his voice calls out. My stomach rolls with revulsion. I don't know who I hate more at this point, him or J. They're stripping us of our dignities, as well as our clothes. I want to spit in their faces and tell them to eat a bag of dicks.

After another minute, I feel a tugging on my jeans. I start to struggle to pull away but feel hands clamp down on my legs. "If you don't want me to slice this pretty alabaster skin with these shears, you'll stop struggling," Marcus hisses at me.

When he goes back to cutting after a moment, I kick out with my right foot. Judging by the groan I receive, I make contact with his no-no squares. A minute into my gloating and trying to kick out again, I feel a fist crash into my stomach. It knocks the wind out of me, and Cammie screams.

The bag over my head is ripped off and I come face-to-face with a livid Marcus. Despite the pain and urgent need to gasp for breath, I smile serenely at him. This enrages him and he grabs my shirt by the neck and yanks hard, ripping it right from my body, and leaves me standing in nothing but my bra and tattered pants. He then takes me by the throat and holds me with enough pressure I start to go black around the edges of my vision. He uses his other hand to rip off the rest of my pants. Somewhere in the background, I can hear Cammie begging him to let me go, to stop. Finally, when I start to lose consciousness, he releases my throat, and cool blissful air flows into my starved lungs. This time, I really do gasp for breath.

He's grinning at me lecherously, leering at the exposed parts of my body, so I stare him down, not giving up my dignity for even a moment. He turns with the mound of clothing he gathered from myself and Cammie and tosses them in a garbage bag. While we stare at him he takes a lighter from his pocket and sets the bag ablaze and tosses it outside the truck. He winks at me and my heart sinks. He stalks back over and grabs me by the hair at the nape of my neck, then moves as if to kiss me. So, I do the thing I've wanted to do this whole time and spit right in his face. He roars and a fist collides with my face. My head snaps to the side. The whole right side of my face starts to burn; then, after a moment, the pain registers and I can feel blood trickle down my nose. Even so, I grin at him, taunting him.

"Enough. Back in the cab, Marcus. *Now!*" J's raised voice reaches us. Marcus stills, then glares at me for a long minute, his hands clenching and unclenching, like he wants to continue to use me as a punching bag. "*Now, you little fuck!*" J yells again.

I lean in as close as the cuffs stretching my arms above my

head will allow. "Run along like a good little lapdog, Marco. Master calls," I sneer low enough to only reach his ears.

"I'll be the one to slice you up real nice in the end, bitch, just like J did your friend. Maybe she'll be waiting in heaven for you. What a sweet reunion that will be," he replies in a menacing tone, then he turns and stalks away, shouldering past J standing at the edge of the compartment. They argue quietly for a moment, then I see Marcus's shoulders stiffen and he runs off, leaving J alone with a cowering Cammie and a bleeding me. Let me tell you, I'm not winning any beauty pageants by this point.

"Are you trying to get yourself killed, baby? Marcus isn't very bright. He talks with his fists, and he knows nothing about when to keep girls alive and unmarked to fetch the highest price. I've done a lot of thinking. After I have my fun with you, I know a drug lord in Colombia in the market for a new slave," J tells me, as he walks over to Cammie. "After all, I already have my number-one girl here. Isn't that right, Camisole?" J adds, practically cooing at Cammie, who is visibly shrinking away.

"Do you just talk to hear your own voice or do you really feel so self-important you can't give anyone else around you any peace?" I grit out, my voice hoarse from the choking I received. "Can't you just leave us alone and go play with your boyfriend in the cab of the truck? Maybe compare dick sizes to prove who is indeed smaller?"

"Careful, baby, my hospitality only lasts so far. I'm feeling particularly violent, and you wouldn't want me to do something to you and make Cammie watch, or vice versa, would you?" he sneers. I close my mouth so hard my teeth snap together. "I didn't think so. It doesn't matter. I look forward to having you and breaking you when we get to our destination. I hope you ladies like Texas. We'll be there shortly."

With that, he turns on his heel and walks to the edge of the truck, and jumps out. With a wink, he seals us inside.

"Auntie Z, you're a badass. But you don't look so good," Cammie calls out to me. I lift my head and see her sweet face up close for the first time. Well, as much as I can see with one eye starting to swell closed. She looks enough like Collin that it makes my heart ache.

"This ain't nothing, Cammie, my dear. You should hear about the black eye I gave to Officer Sparky back in St. Louis that your uncle sicced on me. He can be such a jerkface," I tell her, trying to make light of the situation.

"Do you love my uncle, Auntie Z, is that why you're here?" Cammie asks quietly.

I pause for a moment, wondering what I should say, but in the situation we're in, there's not much room for dishonesty, though I still try to be mindful to the cameras and microphones surrounding us. "Yes, Cammie, I do love him. But I'm not here for him, I'm here for you. Ever since he told me he was going to try to find you, I wanted to be here. I wanted you to know somebody understands and somebody who never even met you was going to fight for you. I might not be winning right now, but I'm still going to fight like hell for you."

"Thank you, Auntie Z. Can you tell me about Sparky now?" she exclaims. I smile over at her. She really is a champ, and we're getting out of this. Alive.

"Why certainly, but the first thing you absolutely need to know, is that no man is ever allowed to pull a lady's hair. Not unless he buys her dinner first, and asks very nicely. Or else, you have full rights to pop up and ninja his ass. Got me?" I say sassily, and she giggles.

"I may or may not have stolen your uncle's wallet, which is why Officer Sparky started chasing me. But you know how St. Louis streets are, your uncle was most likely mistaken. After all, do I really look like the type to steal from anyone?" I give her my best innocent look, which apparently, with the blood leaking all over me, doesn't work that well, and her giggles continue. "But let's talk about you. Before this mess, were there any boys you liked at school, or was there any subject at school you couldn't wait to go to?" I ask, trying to keep her mind off the fucked-up situation we're currently in, just to keep her talking.

"Well, I was really good at science, you can ask my mom, and I won the science fair three years in a row. I kinda liked Caleb Monroe, but he didn't even know I was alive," she tells me nonchalantly.

"Go on, tell me more. I want to know all that is Cammie Reeves."

THIRTY-SIX

COLLIN

"Uh, Lieutenant, we have a problem." Kaysen's voice pulls me from my own musings as I stare out at the darkened highway. I turn my head and see his grim expression and my inner alarm raises at his face. He keeps glancing at the road, then at his phone, and then me, causing me to begin to panic. The miles between us and Zaydra seem to stretch even longer with every minute she's been taken. We're a few hours into driving, and it seems like these people just keep staying ahead of us, no matter how fast we go.

"What is it?" I ask urgently, trying to mentally brace myself for whatever bad news Kaysen is about to impart on me. The universe seems to be stacked against us tonight.

"Zaydra's tracker just went offline somewhere in between Baton Rouge and the Texas state line. It wasn't moving for a good fifteen minutes, and I thought they had stopped and we were going to catch up to them, but then the tracker went dark. They must have found it. They could know we're on to them," Kaysen divulges angrily.

Fuck, this isn't good. If we can't track them, then we have no earthly idea where they're going.

"Wait. If they usually operate out of big cities, like New

Orleans, we can garner that they'll try to hide amongst another big city with a lot of crime, right? New Orleans...what about Houston? It coincides with the way they were heading. It's possible, right?" Jensen muses suddenly. You can see everyone's minds whirling, trying to come up with anything else. It does make sense though.

"They do have ties to the cartel in Mexico, and we all know that the cartel is heavily dominant in Houston and Dallas. Texas would be a logical place to take the girls, to restart a trafficking ring. High crime rate, a lot of gang violence, and cartel activity. It would be a great place to hide in plain sight," I announce to the men, praying we're not wrong. I turn to Kaysen. "We head to Houston. That's our new base for operations at this point." I move my head to lock eyes with Ryan. "Update the Feds on what just happened and what our theory is. If they have any better theories or ideas, they can send them our way. They know we're not trying to get vigilante justice, but if they don't start helping with this, I'm going to stop our updates. Understood?"

He nods sharply and pulls out his phone again to make more calls. After repeating what I said verbatim to the Feds, he goes quiet, nodding occasionally at what the other person is saying. After several minutes, Ryan throws out a terse goodbye and presses the end button. He glances up at me. "The Feds think our theory is plausible. They're trying to trace any cell data that pings off the tracker and the same tower in the same vicinity. So far, they have thousands; after all, it's the interstate. They are still digging and will call us back with more information when they have it.

"There will be agents that will meet us in Houston to coordinate with us. Houston P.D. has also been alerted, to be on the lookout for any suspicious activity having to do with any females. Cammie's photograph is being circulated, as well as Zaydra's description. If these guys are running with them, we're finding them. They're not going to get far." The conviction in his voice eases my panic slightly, and I nod once to my oldest friend in understanding.

"Any word on Amber yet?" I ask him in a low voice. He just shakes his head and looks out the window. I know it's killing him to be here with me and not there with her. As his friend, I appreciate his sacrifice. The silence stretches on and I can't take it anymore. So, I take a deep breath and do the only thing I can think to do in this situation.

"Oh, baby, baby, how was I supposed to know?" I belt out and pause for dramatic effect to the chorus of male groans in the SUV. "That something wasn't right here," I continue, to everyone's chagrin. It keeps them level-headed and my head out of the darkness that threatens to consume me. By the glares I'm getting, these men don't appreciate my musical concert, though. "What, guys, everyone knows Britney is the Queen," I say indignantly.

"Just because some girl named Lindsey told you that during high school doesn't mean we have to be tortured with nineties pop music," Anderson exclaims and Jensen snickers. They all apparently remember the story from years ago. I'm about to start belting out more Britney when we hear a buzzing sound. Ryan pulls out his phone and quickly reads his screen. After he finishes, he lets the phone fall to the seat and exhales loudly.

"She made it through surgery, she's in ICU recovery. She's going to have some deep scarring, but she's alive," Ryan reveals after a moment.

A cheer goes up from the men throughout the car, and Ryan looks ten years older than our twenty-nine years. That's the first bit of good news we've gotten all night. Maybe luck is finally turning our way. I'd pray to every god out there and possibly sell my immortal soul if it got both of my girls back, safe and sound. I glance at Kaysen, whose eyes are glued to the endless highway in front of him.

"As fast as you can get us there, Kavanaugh. We need to get my girls."

He presses the accelerator to the floor and gives me a two-fingered salute. The SUV eats up the miles and I feel the urge to kill these abductors increase with every passing mile. I smile grimly to myself because, for these men, I'm about to become judge, jury, and executioner.

THIRTY-SEVEN

COLLIN

ONCE WE REACH HOUSTON, WE DECIDE TO TOUCH BASE with the federal agents. Ryan calls them to coordinate where to meet and they decide on the downtown safe house where the agents are staying. Kavanaugh angles the SUV towards downtown as Ryan barks directions at him. All of the men are anxious to get out of this vehicle and do something. Helpless is not a good feeling for us. We finally pull into a small nondescript driveway. The house itself looks more like a soccer mom lives here rather than a team of federal agents going in and out, but when you're a part of the federal government, you can give off any illusion you want.

We all exit the vehicle and make our way up the driveway as the door opens, revealing two men. I walk up the steps first and set my gaze on the agents. They step aside to allow us to walk past. Once all the men are inside, the door shuts. The larger of the two agents extends his hand for a handshake, which I immediately take.

"Lieutenant, we've heard good things. I'm Agent McCall and this is my partner, Agent Rosenthal. We're here on behalf of the bureau. We understand you have been tracking the same trafficking ring you busted three years ago. Do you know why they would specifically target people close to you?" Agent McCall questions, looking at me with serious eyes. As an older agent, I imagine he's seen a lot of situations like this. His partner is younger, looks a little greener, but has the silent type thing down to a T. He's just staring at me intensely.

"I've been wracking my brain with that same question for six months, ever since my niece got snatched in St. Louis. The only reasons I could think of would be two. It's either money motivated—I recently made my fortune, as I'm sure you know, with private security and online deciphering—or it's personal. I was the one who put the bullet in their leader.

"But the second option doesn't make sense. These types of men don't have personal vendettas, they're bottom feeders in this society. They don't exactly build rapports with each other, and they use fear and loathing to lead. It makes no sense that this would be personal."

McCall nods his understanding. "In my experience, this is usually monetarily motivated, but they haven't sent a ransom, in, you said, the six months they've had your niece. And now you said they took a woman you are involved with, correct?" He shoulders on with his questioning and at my nod he continues. "Then we need to consider that this is personal to their leader. What do you know about the previous leader—Gonzales, wasn't it?"

"I know he was connected to the cartel, he was connected to human slave traders overseas, but honestly, after the death of Senator Thornhill's daughter, we didn't dig any deeper. The recon was done for us. We were sent in for extraction that was it," I respond tightly, knowing my team should have done more due diligence, and that has always haunted me. Finally, McCall nods and waves us inside the living room to be seated. We must have passed whatever test that was. Rosenthal marches over to the computer that is set up, and sits down, his fingers flying quickly over the keyboard.

"What's on the laptop?" I intone to the agent. He spares me one glance and stares back at the monitor.

"He's tracking a truck we think the girls were transported in. He was reviewing traffic light camera footage from around the house you said Zaydra was taken from, and the warehouse, and one tractor trailer is seen in both areas. The registration goes back to someone who has legally been dead five years, so for now, it's our best lead. Right before you showed, Rosenthal called and sent a nationwide APB out on the plates and the tractor trailer. It's not much, but right now it's what we have," McCall tells me from his seated position.

"Does your partner not speak?" I growl at him.

Rosenthal's hands pause on the keyboard. "His partner speaks when the situation calls for it, but I figured you'd rather me use my brain to find your woman, or was I mistaken?" Rosenthal says in a guttural voice. His vocal chords are obviously messed up, but I feel properly chastised.

"Of course. You're right, I'm sorry. It's just been an incredibly long night. We're all on edge here. We just want the girls back, and to stop the son of a bitch responsible. That's the end goal for all of us." My response is soft but firm. He meets my gaze over his monitor, and nods once.

"Understood. Now stop hovering like a mother hen and let me work," he grunts out. Shaking my head, I make my way over to a recliner across from my men's position on the couches.

McCall clears his throat, and says quietly, "His vocal chords were damaged in Fallujah when he was a Marine. He doesn't like to talk about it. Or to talk much in general. You get used to it, and I've always been a talker anyway."

Understanding dawns on me and I feel like even more of an ass. I'm certainly not making any friends today. Zaydra would laugh her ass off at me having to apologize more than once a night. I'd let her steal from me again if she was here, anything she wanted. I sigh at my own thoughts, steeling myself against all emotion.

"I'd sell my left nut for some food right now," Miguel announces to the group. McCall just laughs and rises from his seated position. He walks out of the room for two minutes, only to return with boxes of pizza. All the men groan at once.

"I figured you guys might be hungry after driving all night. We bought some pizza and soda, or water is in the kitchen. No alcohol. Rosenthal and I are on duty, sorry," McCall states as he sets the boxes down on the coffee table and my men fall on them like wolves. I just roll my eyes and jump into the fray.

THIRTY-EIGHT

ZAYDRA

THE TRUCK STOPS MOVING AFTER WHAT FEELS LIKE A million years. The doors to the back of the compartment open and both J and Marcus are standing there. Marcus gives me an evil glare and walks over to Cammie. He unlatches her chain from the truck and jerks her along, leading her out of the truck. All the while, I'm straining and hissing curses at him. J saunters over and unlatches my chain from the truck. He starts to lead me out like a dog on a leash, and I dig my heels in, to where he is practically dragging me out of the container we're in. Realizing this is getting me nowhere and only wasting my energy, I stop fighting him. He glances back at me with a surprised look on his face.

I just glower at him and he shakes his head, the ice-cold back in his eyes. He leads me to a large three-story building, where the only light is the one busted streetlight occasionally flickering in a yellow glow. If there was one building that ever screamed "danger, keep out," it's this one, especially since I see the grave-yard across the way. I've never been good at scary movies—I always yelled at the characters and got kicked out of the movie theater I was squatting in. I have half a mind to try to escape right now, just because I don't want to go in there.

Against my will, J leads me inside, where I see dozens of females, in various states of dress and all different ages, probably up to thirty. All of them have that terrified, hungry look I've come to associate with homelessness and hopelessness, only these girls are being trafficked. Some of the older ones look strung out, and my heart just breaks at the empty looks a few of them are giving me. So many faces, I want to cry. I see over a dozen men, who all call out to J and make lewd comments about me and my body. Trying to muster what dignity I still have, I straighten and walk straight-backed behind my captor, not deigning to look at any of these men. Like I'm a princess, like none of them matter, because they don't. I'm getting us out of this, somehow.

I'm led straight into a room on the second floor, where I see Cammie on the mattress in one corner, chained to the floor. She's got a bruise blooming on one cheek, and I see tears sparkle in her eyes. I turn and hiss at Marcus who just smirks my way and blows me a kiss while he leans against the wall. I spit at his feet and he straightens. There's a tug on the chain and I turn my head to see J attaching it to the same metal piece Cammie's is attached to.

"After a while, Marcus is going to come in here to take you to bathe, because I'd rather not fuck you when you're covered in blood and dirt. Don't fight him, or, like I told you before, you'll be watching me with Camisole," J says coldly, as he faces us. I grit my teeth angrily and stare him down, not bothering with a response. After a moment, they both stride out, leaving me and Cammie alone.

As soon as the men are out of sight, she runs and ducks underneath my chain, then collapses in my arms and starts to sob. I make soothing noises while I hold her tight as much as I can with us both chained, not knowing what to say to make this better. After a while, her cries start to subside and I lead her to the mattress for her to lie down. Once I get her settled, she almost instantly falls asleep, having cried her energy all out.

I make my way over to the wall, or as far as my chain will

allow, so I can access the strengths and weaknesses of this room. One of their mistakes was leaving my legs unchained; I can do a lot of damage if given the chance. I silently make my way around the room, my eyes bouncing off everything in the room. I take in the fact the floor is concrete, and besides the metal rung in the floor that we're tethered to, the only other thing in the room are the two mattresses. The frustration in me starts to rise. Just then, the door clangs open and Marcus steps through the doorframe. At the intrusion, Cammie sits straight up with wild eyes.

"Miss me, ladies?" Marcus says snarkily, stepping in to the tiny room.

"Like a cat misses a hairball, or better yet, like your mom misses you," I respond sweetly. He starts towards me and stops, takes a deep breath, and composes himself. "Boss isn't letting me hit you again, or else I won't get paid. Can't damage the merchandise, but there's other ways to torture you bitch," he utters evilly, then stalks to Cammie and yanks her up by her hair. At her cry, I shoot to my feet. He proceeds to wrap her long auburn locks around his fist and cruelly yank. The more she fights, the harder he pulls. She's screaming and crying, trying to yank free, to no avail. He then raises his other fist.

"All right! Stop it, you fuck. I'll quit. Cammie, sweetheart, I'm sorry."

He releases Cammie, who cowers back from him, clutching her head. She just looks at me with tears swimming in her eyes and she nods. As Marcus turns to walk to me, Cammie mouths, "He's got a gun," and I feel my alarm increase. Calmly, I nod back at her, letting her know everything is going to be all right. He reaches me and pulls me up roughly by the chain, my aching wrists screeching in protest at the movement. Marcus proceeds to unlock me from my chains and put his gun to my temple. The blood in my veins freezes. I'm struggling with my "fight or flight" instincts.

"Let's get you showered. Nobody likes a crusty bitch," he

rumbles at me. I roll my eyes but start to walk. We make it just outside the doorway. "Go right. It's that first door."

I do what he says, and we reach a dingy bathroom with a tiny shower and toilet. "Take those scraps of lace off now, bitch, and get in the shower. No need to be modest, you aren't that much to look at," he taunts from behind me. With my mustered courage, I take off my bra and panties and step under the showerhead, only for it to give me a blast of cold water. I let out a shriek, and I hear him laugh. "Oh, did I forget to mention there isn't any hot water? Here's a bar of soap."

He chucks a bar of soap at my head. Thankfully, my reflexes are returning after the blow to the head. I catch it in one hand, and start to take the fastest shower of my life. When I finally step out of the shower, dripping water all over the floor, I'm shaking so bad from the cold. Marcus is just looking at me with hate in his eyes and no trace of pity.

I take a step towards him when he beckons me forward, and I slip on the excess water, crashing directly into him. He makes a disgusted sound in the back of his throat, and straightens me, groping all over my body as he does. "You fucking soaked my clothes, you dumb bitch. I don't know why he brought you along. He should just let us all fuck you and kill you, and be done with it." The hatred in his tone is palpable.

"Maybe if you had given me a towel, I wouldn't be soaking wet. And stop groping me. I'd rather be felt up by my great aunt who used to remark on how big I'd gotten. Also, kindly fuck off," I say, unable to hold back my sass anymore.

A sharp slap to the face tells me it was the wrong move. He brings out his gun and puts it right between my eyes. At this point, I feel like I'm staring down my death. He must see the fear in my eyes because after a moment, he smiles and throws a towel from behind him in my face. It isn't much bigger than a washcloth but it does the trick, and I towel off quickly. He lets me redress in my underwear—*for now*, he says. He then has me lead him back to the room, a gun pressed to the back of my head the whole time.

Once back inside with Cammie, he chains me up again and tells me tersely, "When the time comes, bitch, I will so enjoy killing you. Until then, wait for the boss. He'll be by soon to sample the goods." He gives me an evil grin and stalks to the open door, slamming it behind him.

Cammie, whose tears have dried while I was gone, looks at me and waits for me to say something, to let her know what just happened. I say nothing, but raise my hand enough to show her the light glinting off the keys I lifted from Marcus when I crashed into him. Her eyes fill with hope, and I give her the universal shushing motion. If there's anyone listening, I don't want them to hear what I just borrowed. After all, everyone knows you can't trust a pickpocket.

THIRTY-NINE

COLLIN

"Gentlemen, we got a hit on the tractor trailer. It was spotted near a row of buildings across from Martha Chapel Cemetery. We heard nothing about women, but if this truck is near any abandoned buildings, these are our guys," Rosenthal says gutturally.

"Did you say Martha Chapel Cemetery?" Miguel asks his voice shaking slightly. At Rosenthal's nod, he says, mostly to himself, "Of course they would be on Demon's Road, *Dios Mio*, of course they would be. *Mi abuela* says that is where a man goes to get possessed."

"Miguel, I don't care if I have to fight demons, ghosts, pedophiles or zombies out for my brains, I'll channel Dean Winchester then because I'm going and getting the girls," I say through gritted teeth. He still looks at me, nervous, but he nods. "Anybody else have a problem going and checking these buildings out?"

Everyone shakes their heads. Good, I don't have time for superstitions when these assholes have had Zaydra going on twelve hours.

McCall makes his way over to me and claps me on the shoulder. "This isn't the easiest thing, but why don't you let me take the lead on this one. I have a team of men waiting on my orders."

"With all due respect, that isn't your woman or your blood in there. It's mine. This is my operation. Your men can join in if you want, but it's my command. My men and I have done this before; many times, in fact. We're a well-oiled machine. Your help would be appreciated, but if it comes down to it, it's not needed. I'm doing this with or without you," I respond in the same soft, commanding tone.

"Understood, Lieutenant, you'll take the lead, but my men will be on scene to execute search and rescue for these females," McCall says, understanding, and I just nod my thanks. I move to the front door, with my men hot on my heels, when McCall's voice stops me. "If your girls are there, Reeves, you need to steel yourself to the fact that things might not go the way you plan. Any number of things could go wrong, so just be prepared."

Thank you, Mr. Positivity. Without a word, I stalk out to the SUV. Murphy's Law can kiss my ass tonight.

We all get loaded up. I let Miguel take the wheel this time, since he seems to know where he's going without the use of a map. He's cursing quietly to himself in Spanish, and doesn't seem to be keen on going to this area, but we have no choice. The agents are following behind us in a black, nondescript sedan. A blanket of calm settles over me and I take a deep breath. All my men seem to be doing the same. We need clear heads for everything if we're about to face off with a pedophilic ring…again.

FORTY

ZAYDRA

I UNLOCK CAMMIE FIRST AND SHE HUGS ME AROUND THE
neck, then I unlock myself from the chains, and rub my wrists
to ease the rawness. Getting free from the chains was the easy
part. Now, I just have to figure out how to get Cammie and I
out of this building without getting shot or recaptured. My
mind is racing with all the routes to points of exit I saw on the
way up here, and where the girls were downstairs and where the
men were posted up. There are a lot of potential risks in trying
to escape, but I'm not going to lay here and do nothing, and
allow myself to be raped. Never again.

I'm whispering to Cammie, quietly and urgently, when I
hear loud footsteps outside the room. I urge Cammie back on
her mattress facing the wall, with the chain draped over her like
it's still attached, and I do the same to myself. The door
screeches open, and I hear soft male chuckles.

"Pretending to be asleep, are we, sweet Zaydra? You know
that won't save you," J tells me in hushed tones. He comes closer,
and I'm glad I made the choice to drape the towel I had over my
hands with the chain underneath, because while my near naked-
ness leaves me vulnerable, it wasn't blatantly obvious I was

unchained. I just need to surprise J to overpower him. We'll never make it otherwise.

I start to tremble, the mattress shaking enough, it alerts him I'm awake. He chuckles again, and I feel the mattress dip with the weight of his knees. Right when he's about to reach for me and I prepare to pop up and ninja his ass, I hear a small battle cry, and Cammie jumps on his neck with her chain wrapped around him tightly, as if she's going to strangle him.

It shocks J enough that he straightens, and I jump up and punch him twice in the dick. He lets out a choked groan as he claws frantically behind him, trying to get Cammie off his back. He twists away from me, trying to throw her off, and I see the gun in his belt. I grab for it quickly with all the skill I have, so he doesn't feel it missing. He finally throws Cammie off by her hair and twists around to face me with a snarl, to see his gun pointed right between his eyes. J stops cold and his eyes narrow. I feel a smile stretch my face wide, to the point where I'm sure I look like a deranged muppet—way worse than my deranged beauty queen of old.

"What are you going to do, shoot me?" J intones menacingly, and I simply continue to smile.

"Maybe," I tell him with raised brows, my tone mocking. "Maybe I'll let her do it." I cock my head towards Cammie. "Or maybe I'll take you downstairs by gunpoint and execute you in front of your men, to assert *my* dominance, because Lord knows that's what these men respond to."

J just stares at me with an expressionless face, and I make sure I'm not close enough where he can jerk the gun from my hands before I shoot him. I give him a finger twirl, indicating what I had decided, and my mind races. I don't want to shoot him, but maybe I can bargain with these men for our release. If not, we'll go down, guns blazing.

"Let's go, J, I don't want to be with you one second more. Your presence makes me itch, like crabs. Besides, I need to go let your men know who's in charge, so I can get back to my man."

"You know, he took everything from me." I must give him a blank stare because he continues on. "Your man, Collin," J spits out, "took every fucking thing from me." I give him a disbelieving look, and motion towards the door. "He killed my brother! The only family I fucking had left. Shot him because of some stupid *puta.* The funny thing is, Carlos never trafficked that girl; the dumb whore was addicted to drugs before she met Carlos. He dealt to her once, and she decided to run away from Daddy, and come here to be my brother's queen. It was her idea to start trafficking other girls to pay for her drug habit. She would have died for my brother. In the end, she did, happily.

"My name was Julio then, and I was the bodyguard for my brother, but I was out getting new girls when shit went down. But your fucking man didn't bother to find out the facts before he put my brother down like a dog. I'm the heir to this throne of death and sex, thanks to Collin. If anybody is truly to blame for both of you being kidnapped, it's him. He took from me, so I had to take from him," he finishes and stares at me with crazy eyes.

He springs at me, taking me by surprise. The whole time he had been talking, he was inching closer without my knowledge. He grabs for the gun and dislodges my finger from the trigger, but neither of us has a good grip on it, so I headbutt him, causing him to stumble away from me. Forgetting nobody wins with a headbutt, I drop the gun and it clatters to the ground. Momentarily disoriented, we both stand there, dazed.

As our senses return, he jumps towards me, hitting me in the face. At that moment, I hear a loud *crack,* and feel something wet spray my face. J's eyes glaze over and he crumples to the ground with less grace than you see in movies, revealing Cammie, standing there with a smoking gun in her hand.

"You said if anybody ever yanked me by the hair again, I could pop up and ninja them. Well, he threw me off by the hair. That counts, right?" Cammie exclaims, near hysterics.

"Yeah, baby, that counts. Here, sweetheart, give me the gun.

One of the men was bound to hear that downstairs. We gotta go, and I mean, we gotta go right now," I tell her quickly. She nods her understanding, but doesn't take her eyes off the limp J on the floor. "He's not going to hurt you again."

A single tear falls down her face before her eyes lift to meet mine. She hands me the gun.

"Okay, Auntie Z, let's go home," she whispers.

FORTY-ONE

COLLIN

THERE ARE ABOUT SIX BUILDINGS OUT THIS WAY, AND EACH one looks like the last. There are no men in front any of them, which is expected. Keeping a low profile in a place like this wouldn't be too hard, but the first rule as always, is to never show what you have, just like in cards. We're all sitting in the SUV, perusing the buildings, trying to discern which one contains the girls. We don't want to chance picking the wrong one and tip them off if we go inside. I left the heat signature goggles in my Range Rover, so we're relying on the research of the buildings before we go inside. The interior of the cab is quiet, except for our breathing. I turn to acknowledge the men, one by one, to make sure their minds are right before they follow me into hell, again.

All the men give me a slight nod to let me know they're still with me, except Miguel, who's staring out the window on his side, straight at the graveyard that takes up the other side of the road. Miguel's lips are moving but no sound is escaping.

"Miguel, what are you doing?" I ask after a moment of watching him.

"I'm praying that my ass doesn't get possessed in this evil place. Please, God, let the demons take the pretty boy. The ladies would miss me too much if I got possessed, so take one for the team, Jensen, okay?" Miguel replies, as his superstitions get the best of him.

"What the hell? Why do I need the devil to get me? If anybody gets possessed, it's going to be Malcolm. I've heard a lot of girls call him the devil," Jensen whisper-shouts to Miguel.

"Nah, dude, they said I had that devil dick, the good-good. You'll get there one day, bud, we all believe in you," Malcolm replies in an even tone to Jensen, who glares between him and Miguel.

Anderson and Ryan just shake their heads and roll their eyes, knowing they're using the light bickering to mask any apprehension they may have. I cock my head at them and give them a look. The men sober up quickly, and Ryan's phone buzzes once more.

Ryan reads his phone. "McCall said that Rosenthal found that the building on the far left is owned by a Ventrilia Farm Equipment, LLC, but the problem is that there is no Ventrilia Farm Equipment, LLC. The rest are legit. It looks like that's them."

"The cartel must own the building. There's no way these men have that kind of money, and if they do, that's news to all of us. We seized all of the assets last time. That being said, it's likely to be crawling with men as well as the trafficked girls. Don't shoot a friendly, get the girls out quick. If you have to put the men down, do so, but only if your life is in immediate danger—otherwise, subdue. Let's go fuck their night up, gentlemen, shall we?" I growl.

On cue, the men all exit the SUV, quietly and efficiently. We all arm up for the second time tonight, and as we finish strapping down, McCall and Rosenthal make their way to us with vests of their own that say "FBI."

"Tactical is three minutes out. We called it in the moment we found the dummy LLC. documentation. They'll wait for my command to enter, and in turn, I'll wait for yours, Lieutenant."

At my nod, we start the silent creep forward to the building. Using hand motions, I keep the men a few paces behind me, with Ryan to my immediate left. We walk in unison, stalking silently towards the building that becomes more ominous as we get closer. The moment we get close enough, we see dim lighting coming from the second-floor window. Knowing we are only going to get one shot to get everyone out safely, I take a deep breath and pray Zaydra and Cammie are alive and unhurt, and that these men burn in hell for their crimes.

I nonverbally tell the men to hold their position to wait for the tactical unit, needing all the men we can get. Suddenly, a shot rings out on the second floor and we hear multiple female screams. My heart jumps to my throat, and I react. I'm in the door before I know what I'm doing, with my AK aimed in front of me. My sudden entrance into the building does not go unnoticed. There are multiple voices yelling and women and girls huddle together in the corner as the first shot rings out.

Everything goes to hell, just as I predicted. There are young girls running for cover, while at least twenty men pull out weapons and engage. Some of them use little girls as cover, and Malcolm takes those men out first, one by one, until the tactical team enters the building behind us. The remaining men standing start to panic and their shooting becomes more sporadic. My eyes are scanning the whole room, through the smoke from the weapons, looking for Zaydra or Cammie, and my heart rate increases with each passing face not being theirs. I motion for Ryan to take the lead in subduing the men while I search for my girls.

I'm squatting down, looking at all the cowering faces, when I hear, "Collin!" My head jerks up to see Zaydra on the second floor, staring down at me in nothing but her bra and panties. She's smiling and tears are streaming down her face as she starts towards me.

A moment later, Cammie's face comes into view and I feel a punch to my gut. After all these months, she's alive. I feel a tear track down my cheek. I start for them, to meet them halfway, before I remember the firefight still happening at the moment. I quickly turn to look at the fray and am relieved to see multiple men on their knees with their hands behind their heads, weapons on the ground, with SWAT standing above them, weapons drawn. My eyes find McCall and he inclines his head for me to go get my woman. I grin at him, and turn back to see Cammie running at me. I catch her in my open arms and twirl her around.

"Uncle Collin," Cammie chokes out through her tears. "I didn't know if you would come."

My eyes dart up to find Zaydra, and they widen in horror. Coming towards me is Marcus, with a hand around Zaydra's throat and a gun to her head.

"Camisole, baby girl, get behind me. Go to Uncle Ryan. *Right. Now,*" I whisper to Cammie quickly, and she does what I say without question. "Let her go, Marcus, you're outnumbered here," I tell him loudly.

"I think not. This bitch is my ticket out of here. We both know you won't chance a shot with my gun to her head. Wouldn't want to gamble her life, would you? Now, give me the keys to your vehicle. Princess here is coming with me," Marcus roars at us, spittle flying from his mouth.

Zaydra is staring at me with wide eyes, trying to communicate with me. Her eyes bore into mine, and she darts her gaze down to Marcus's arm before glancing back up to me. I give her a barely perceptible nod and she mouths, "On three" to me.

I bare my teeth at Marcus. "I think not, fucker. *Three!*" I yell out and Zaydra slumps forward with all her weight, breaking the hold Marcus has on her enough that I squeeze my trigger and his body flies backwards, the gun clattering uselessly to the ground.

Without hesitation, Zaydra flies towards me and jumps into my arms, locking her legs around my waist. She hugs my neck, like she's afraid I'll disappear. "If this is what it takes to get your legs around me, I should have shot somebody a long time ago," I whisper in her ear.

"This is me distracting you, so I can steal your wallet again. It went so well for me the first time, I promised myself if I got the chance again, this time, I would climb you like a tree," she murmurs in reply, smiling against my neck.

I hug her back for a good two minutes before I lower her to her feet. I whirl around, dragging Zaydra by the hand, and stride towards Ryan, who is using his body to shield Cammie from the gruesome images around us. One of the FBI agents brings Zaydra some clothing and I'm grateful. The sweatpants and T-shirt, too large for her, are a million times better than seeing her in her lingerie with all these people around.

"No friendly fatalities," Ryan declares and I acknowledge his statement with a jerk of my chin. I motion him to the side, and upon seeing Cammie's tear-soaked face, I wrap her in my arms.

"I would never forget about you, Cammie. You're the reason I'm here. My favorite girl. I'm so sorry it took me this long to find you. I'm here now, honey. I won't let anything bad happen ever again. I love you, Camisole," I utter firmly, my voice hoarse with unshed tears. "We have to get you home to your mom. She's going crazy looking for you." Cammie just buries her face more into my arm and trembles. I look at Zaydra at my side. "So, Marcus was J the whole time?"

She shakes her head. "J is upstairs, with a bullet in him. He was Carlos's brother, and hated you for taking his brother from him," Zaydra replies, and proceeds to tell me what J told her about the senator's daughter. For a moment, we're all dumbfounded by the tale she relays to us. I rub Cammie's back soothingly as her sobs start to subside, my mind whirling. I try to make sense of how we could have been given such wrong information.

"Did you shoot the bastard?" I ask after a moment, and Zaydra slowly shakes her head at me. Her eyes slide to the girl in my arms, who's cried herself to sleep.

"She shot him, after he tried to rape me. Collin…he really did a number on her. She's not the same kid she was six months ago, I guarantee it," Zaydra tells me, causing my heart to break for my niece. I place a soft kiss on her head.

"She can be whoever she wants to be when she's home. We're going to get her the help she needs. I'm so glad I taught her to shoot. I'm so glad you found each other. I'm so glad I found you."

Zaydra gives me a tired smile, then focuses on the men being led out of the building in cuffs by the FBI. She glances back at me, confused. "We made some new friends tonight, trying to find you," I say, as I lean in and capture her mouth with mine. I break the kiss after a moment.

"It's always good to have friends in high places, but I'm mostly wondering if I ever pickpocketed any of them while I lived in Virginia," she whispers conspiratorially. My eyes must widen at her because she busts out laughing and Ryan breezes past me, laughing softly. "Ryan," Zaydra calls after him, and he stops and angles his head at her. "Amber… Is she… Is she..."

He smiles at Zaydra slightly. "She's alive. She's out of surgery, in recovery. She's still in ICU, she lost a lot of blood, but we both know she's too stubborn to die." He answers her unspoken question. Zaydra's shoulders visibly sag with her relief, and she just nods as her lip trembles, her eyes bright from a sheen of unshed tears.

"Lieutenant, can we get out of this place? It's giving me hives from all the bad juju," Miguel asks as he rushes towards us. Before he reaches me, he picks Zaydra up and twirls her once before dropping her back to her feet. "By the way, *pequeña belleza*, if you want to pick my pockets any time, I won't get you kidnapped for your troubles. You can steal my wallet like you stole my heart," he schmoozes, forgetting his fear for all of two seconds, before he looks around and cringes again.

"Aww, well, that's sweet, Miguel, but I stole your watch two minutes ago and you didn't even notice. I'm hurt." At his bewildered look, she holds up his black watch and winks. He looks from her face to his now naked wrist, and then tilts his head back and laughs. She shakes his watch at him and he snatches it from her hands. She laughs as he mockingly glowers at her.

"*Está loca*, Lieutenant, you better be careful. You might end up missing more than your heart if you piss this one off. She'll steal your kidney and sell it just to spite you, without you ever knowing. Now, get me the hell out of here," he says quickly and stalks away.

We start helping the FBI with the remaining women. All my men help get the little ones crouched on the ground, who are scared out of their minds, out the doors and away from the gruesome scene, into the safety that is awaiting them. McCall and Rosenthal escort them to vehicles to get them to their safe house. I shift Cammie around to cradle her in one arm and take Zaydra's hand as Rosenthal brings the last shaking woman outside to the awaiting trucks.

I lead Zaydra outside to the SUV, which all the men are loading into. Zaydra slides into the passenger seat at my urging and I hand my sleeping niece to Ryan, who straps her in without jostling her. I make my way to the driver's seat, but before I can pull open the door, Rosenthal jogs towards me, handing me his card.

"I'm glad we found your ladies, and that they were alive. We got lucky. Thanks for your help busting this ring. If you and your men want to get into private contracting with the FBI, give us a call. Until next time, Lieutenant," he announces in that guttural voice of his. He then extends his hand, but I surpass his handshake and grip his forearm in a warrior's greeting. He inclines his head to me.

"I don't believe private contracting is in the cards. Security is enough for me, but if you ever need a favor, don't hesitate to ask. Until then, don't hack me," I tell him mockingly. He just smiles and steps back, flipping me off as I climb in the SUV. I start it and when the engine rumbles to life, I look to Zaydra and find her smiling at me.

"I take it you have another bromance going on? I'm having to compete for your affection with way too many dudes. I'm not sure it's worth it," she says, exasperated.

At that, I do the only thing I want to do—I seal my mouth over hers to the chorus of male groans. After our tongues duel for a moment, she breaks the kiss, breathing hard. She leans her forehead against mine and whispers, "Get us home so I can thank you for the rescue properly."

Needing no more prompting, I put the SUV in gear and haul ass out of there.

FORTY-TWO

ZAYDRA

I BLINK MY EYES OPEN BEFORE WE TURN INTO THE GARDEN District. The moment we pull into the driveway in NOLA, a woman comes racing to the SUV and jerks open the back door. Her eyes search the men one by one, until they fall on the still-sleeping Cammie. She then bursts into tears. Collin smiles at her, tired, and I calm the hackles that rose with this stranger running at us.

It takes my tired mind a moment to realize how much Collin and this woman look alike. She has to be Cammie's mom, Collette. Collin must have called her when I passed out early into the trip. I don't know how she got here so fast, but I'm sure if it was my kid, I'd break all kinds of speeding laws to get here too.

Collin gets out of the car and pulls Collette back slightly. He wraps her in a hug while she cries, and she gives him a quick kiss on the cheek before she pulls back and motions for Ryan to give Cammie to her. Cammie's eyes blink open and after a minute, those blue eyes—so like her uncle's and her mom's—focus, and she makes a noise like a wounded animal before she throws herself at her mother. Collette catches her, tears now leaking down both of their faces.

"Thank you, Collin. Thank you. Thank you. Thank you," she whispers to her brother, while rocking Cammie from side to side. She's not a large woman, so the strength she must have to hold up her daughter, who is almost her size, is amazing to me.

"Collette, if you should thank anybody, thank Zaydra. She got taken and kept her safe. She gave Cammie the strength to escape, because when I got there, their escape was almost complete. I just gave them a ride, really," Collin says, smiling at me, completely downplaying his own role in Cammie's rescue. I shake my head lightly at Collette.

"I didn't rescue her, she rescued me. You have a strong daughter; she must take after you and her uncle. She's amazing," I tell Collette, who nods her head with a smile on her face.

"Mama, Auntie Z is right. I ninjaed our way out of there, right, Auntie Z? Mama, you're strangling me!" Cammie cries out, her voice muffled by Collette's tight grip.

Collette looks sheepish for a moment, before loosening her grip enough for the teenager to whirl around and face us, her hand never leaving her mother's. I smile at her fondly, feeling a deep connection to her after everything we've been through.

"Auntie Z?" Collette asks simply.

"Her name is Zaydra, but Uncle Collin sent her to help. I figured that was 'cuz he looooovvveesss her, so she's gotta be my auntie," Cammie replies with humor. The fact she's using humor to keep herself from breaking tells me we have more in common than I thought. What she said takes a minute to register, and when it does, my face flames bright red. I duck my head so I don't lock eyes with Collette, and I hear Collin's laughter. I glare up at him, knowing where the penchant for teasing me that Cammie picked up has come from.

"Ah, I see. Well, let's let your Auntie Z and Uncle Collin go upstairs. They look like they're about to pass out. I want you with me, baby girl. I need to see you're safe, so let's talk. I'll tell you everything you want to know about your dad, I'm sorry I didn't tell you before. I love you, baby. I'm so, so sorry."

Collette leads Cammie into the house as Collin leans in and picks me up, causing me to let out a squeak of surprise. He strides inside the house and bypasses all of his men, goes up the stairs, and deposits me on the bed in the room that was his.

I look up at him from my sprawled situation on the bed and he yanks his shirt off. I prop myself up on my elbows to watch the only show I ever realized I needed to watch. At the sight of his V lines and abs, my mouth goes dry. When he turns to throw the shirt in the corner, his muscles ripple and my pussy spasms. He is the only man capable of doing this to my body. He strings his belt through the loops and locks eyes with me, and the heat that I see in them threatens to set my body on fire. He's stripping so slowly, torturing my body with the delicious sight, but I let him continue because only an idiot would interrupt this show. It's better than any *Magic Mike* dance out there. No offense, but suck it, Channing Tatum.

The moment he pops the button on his jeans and pulls them clean off, with his underwear in tow, I swear my pussy is about to cause me to spontaneously combust, and he hasn't even touched me yet. I realize what he's doing—he's giving me a chance to say no, to tell him I need time. But I don't, I need him, even if I'm self-conscious because I look like a punching bag.

I lift my arms and beckon him to me, and with his straining cock, Collin jumps on me. He grabs my face in his hands and captures my lips for the sweetest kiss. His hands stroke down to my tummy, causing my pussy to clench more, anticipation heating my blood. Next, my T-shirt is up and over my head, and deposited on the ground near his. My sweatpants quickly follow, and as he's undressing me, I'm trying to get my hand around his aching dick, but he keeps batting it away, reminding me of the dream I had when I first met him.

Once he has me fully naked, he sits back on his haunches on the bed and just stares at me. "You're so beautiful, Zaydra. Like some sort of angel the universe pulled straight out of my fantasies," he whispers reverently. I shake my head at him. Knowing the bruises and the scabs he must see on my body, feeling more self-conscious, I go to cover myself but he stops me.

"Never be ashamed of your body. These bruises mean you fought hard, and that's what matters," he tells me, staring into my eyes, then lowers his head to capture my mouth in another scorching kiss. When he breaks it, I'm left panting and aching.

His fingers trace up and over my peaked nipples, teasing my body into a frenzy. His touch is so light, I'm lifting my body up so he'll touch me harder. When he just eases his fingers down my stomach, the wetness in my pussy starts to coat my thighs. I need to be fucked soon, or I'll die. Horniness makes me a dramatic bitch.

Finally, his hand finds the wetness in between my legs when he parts the lips of my pussy, and he lets out a purely masculine groan that sends bolts of ecstasy to my core. I'm about to plead with him when he plunges two fingers into my core, and I cry out. He puts the other hand over my mouth.

"Quiet, baby. My sister and niece are here. Wouldn't want them to know how much you looovveee my cock," he tells me mockingly. I nod and he releases my mouth, while slowly plunging his fingers in and out of my cunt. I can feel the tightening start in my lower belly, and I know it won't be long before I come so hard I scream, so I bite my lip until I taste blood as he increases the speed of his fingers.

The wet sounds my pussy is making would usually embarrass me, but Collin's groans and reverent whispers about how fucking hot I am, and how much he loves my pussy, have me not giving one single fuck. My body tightens to the point of pain I'm trying to breathe through, and I can't seem to orgasm—I'm right on the precipice.

"Come for me, Zaydra," Collin whispers, as he lowers his head and blows cool air lightly on my clit, causing me to come so hard he might as well have drop kicked me over that cliff I was on. I turn my head to moan into the pillow, so the whole house doesn't hear me. Collin eases me down from my orgasm and sits back his heels with a pure male smirk.

I motion him upwards to me, and when he starts to stretch out beside me, I grab his waist with both hands and guide him to straddle my chest. Now, his hard cock right at eye level with my face, and with my pussy still tingling from orgasm, I swipe my tongue over the head to taste the bead of precum that has appeared on the tip. He grunts and catches himself mid-thrust before he tries to fuck my face.

This time, with a purely female smirk, I take his cock in my mouth, without fanfare, trying to take the whole thing down my throat without gagging. He groans loudly, and I allow his cock to pop out. I wink at him and say, "Shhhhh. You wouldn't want your sister and your niece to hear how much you loooooooooovvvvee me, would you?"

When I finish teasing him with my words, I suck his dick back into my mouth, and start to hum. Collin starts cursing and pulls out.

"Evil, witchy woman," he grunts out. Flipping me over so I'm face down on my stomach, he eases my legs apart, and plunges his cock into my aching pussy in one thrust, causing me to scream into the hand he uses to cover my mouth. He sets a punishing pace, jack hammering into my body, until I fly into an intense orgasm without warning. "Yeah, baby, come for me. This is what you wanted when you were sucking me, huh? For me to fuck you hard."

The slapping sounds of skin on skin fills the room, which makes it more erotic. Collin reaches his hand under me and finds my clit. He starts rubbing it in circles while he's pounding into me, causing me to see stars, as my body tightens on the edge of release again. Using my inner muscles, I clamp down on his dick, causing him to curse and lose his rhythm. He lifts my lower body up so only my chest and face are against the mattress, then pulls my legs back around his waist and I can feel him so deep, he's inside my soul at this point. He starts to fuck me like a madman, and I continue to squeeze and release with my inner muscles, milking his dick.

He thrums my clit again, and I go hurtling over the edge, clamping down brutally on his dick, causing him to come. His groan rumbles through his body from his slumped position on my back. It takes us both several minutes to come back down to earth, and he slips out of my body. Collin slumps to the side of me, intending on lying on the bed but missing completely and falling to the floor with a *thump*, causing me to giggle.

After lying there for a minute, I get up on shaky legs, almost like a newborn deer, and make my way to the bathroom. By the time I finish and come back out, he's passed out on the floor. Smiling at the picture before me, I grab two pillows and the blanket from the bed, prop his head up on one, cover us with the blanket, and snuggle down into his chest. Breathing in the scent of us mingled together with the light smell of sex, I relax, and his steady, even breathing lulls me to sleep.

FORTY-THREE

ZAYDRA

Waking to a dark room, I momentarily panic before I realize where I am. I notice I'm in bed alone, when I'm positive we went to sleep on the floor. I search the room but find no trace of Collin. I rise from the bed, and hear his muffled voice coming from the bathroom. Tiptoeing to the door, fully intending on surprising him, I stop cold when I hear, "Mitchell, you're telling me Jason Miller is dead? That he's been dead for a year now? What did the fucker die from?" Collin pauses. "That's way better than how he deserved to go. Did you find anything out about his known associates? Those men he used to preach with?"

My mind is reeling as I step away from the door. My father, my tormentor, is dead? He's been dead a year? I've been to three cities this year alone, running from a man who isn't even alive anymore. Helpless rage fills my body. I've wasted so much of my life running, when I should have just gone to the police and faced this head-on.

I'm angry, so livid right now that when I hear Collin exit the bathroom, I lash out. "You went searching for my fucking father? How dare you? What gives you the right, Collin?" I scream at him. He stares at me with the phone dangling from one hand.

"When it comes to your safety, I would dare a lot of things, Zaydra. I'm not going to apologize for looking into finding a way to make you feel safe," he growls at me. I shake my head at him.

"I can take care of myself, Collin, I always have, and I don't need you to battle my demons for me," I hiss back at him, knowing my anger is mostly directed at myself but not being able to help taking it out on him.

"But I didn't have to battle these demons, Zaydra. He's dead. Your father is dead. He died from a brain aneurysm. It's over. You don't have to run anymore. You can stay right here with me and not be constantly looking over your shoulder. You can do what you want to do with your life, now that you don't have to live in fear of him finding you. You can love me back, like I love you, without worrying about having to leave. You can let me love you," Collin tells me softly, pleading, and it sends a jolt to my heart.

"It's never going to be over for me, Collin! Don't you get that? I'm fucked up. I'm broken, and I don't know if I can ever allow myself to let anybody have that kind of power over me again. I need to go," I choke out, tears filling my eyes.

I rush to the door and make it through when I hear him yell my name. I continue downstairs and my wild eyes find Miguel first. He pauses his strumming of a guitar he must have found somewhere. His eyes meet mine and he straightens immediately.

"What do you need, Zaydra? How can I help?" he asks immediately, not caring if he upsets his old commanding officer. Seeing the sincerity on his face, I almost lose my battle with my tears, but I take a deep breath.

"I need you to take me to see Amber, please," I say softly, feeling one second away from shattering. He nods his consent, and grabs the keys to his SUV. We're out the door before anyone else realizes we're gone. I jump in the passenger's seat as he starts it and puts it in gear. We make it down the drive when I see Collin run outside. I avert my gaze. "Go," I tell Miguel, and he does.

"I don't know what happened, sweetheart, but if you want to talk about it. I'm here and will listen. But I should tell you that I've never seen Lieutenant love anyone as hard as he loves his family, until he met you. Whatever he's done, I know he did it for good reason. He's probably the best man I know, and he would give the shirt off his back to anyone who needed it. I'm probably going to get an ass-chewing when I get back, because he won't know where you are, but, sugar, you might as well be family now. If you feel anything for him, please just think about giving him another chance."

"Miguel, I appreciate your help, I do. But I don't want to talk about him. He didn't do anything wrong, it's me. It's always me. I've stolen enough of his time already. He's trying to fight all of my demons, and I never asked him to. I'll never be normal. I'll remember every single thing he's ever said or done wrong, and he knows that. How can I ever ask someone like him to love someone like me? I'm homeless, and I pickpocket people for a living. I don't even have a high school diploma," I admit, feeling all kinds of ashamed of where I'm at in life, where I let myself end up because of my refusals to face my past trauma head-on.

"Maybe he doesn't want normal. Maybe he never did. He wants to fight your demons because that's the type of man he is. He would never want to take the choice away from you, though. He just wants to ease your burden. I think he loves you because of everything you said, not in spite of it. You're really fucking strong. I don't know half of what you've been through, but I'm in awe of your strength, so I know he loves you because of it. Plus, you're pretty easy on the eyes," he tells me with a wink, and I laugh despite my tumultuous emotions. But I don't respond because there's nothing I can say to that. So, we ride the rest of the way to the hospital in silence.

Miguel drops me at the front door to the inpatient area, and gives me a smile. "I gotta get back before Lieutenant starts climbing the walls. He's called me fifteen times. I'm gonna get a black eye for this, love. So, go see the other crazy girl, get Thelma and Louise back together. Just think about what I said, okay?" He blows me a kiss. I just nod and give him a small smile, shutting the door with a final wave.

Making my way inside the hospital, I feel the nerves in my gut grow, praying Amber is going to be just fine, and that she doesn't hate me for not being able to save her from J. I stop at the information desk. "My friend, Amber James, is in ICU. Can you point me in the right direction? I'm not sure which room is hers."

She starts typing on the computer in front of her and after a couple of minutes lifts her bespectacled eyes, and says, "Well, sweetie, Amber James isn't in ICU. She was moved to a room on the third floor. You can go up to see her, it's room 322, but visiting hours are over in an hour."

I thank her and find my way to the elevator. As I walk down the brightly lit hallway, all I smell is antiseptic and death, and I remember why I hate hospitals—they remind me of my mother's death. I rethink going into Amber's room empty-handed and I grab a bear off an orderly's cart right before I reach Amber's room. I stop at the door when I hear raised voices.

"Why do you have to be so fucking stubborn, Amber? I'm just trying to be here for you, and you won't let me even do that," Ryan says in a raised voice.

"I wonder why, Detective Dickface. I wouldn't be in this hospital bed if it wasn't for you. You practically made me come because I danced for a skeeze once upon a time. I want you to leave. Now!" Amber yells back at him.

I hear cursing and then Ryan stalks out, glancing back once seeing me, and he just shakes his head and starts to walk away. I take a deep breath and decide, fuck it, and go inside anyway. The moment I walk past the bathroom, I see Amber lying in a hospital bed with bandages all over the top half of her body that the hospital gown doesn't quite hide. The snarl falls off her face when she sees it's me and she bursts into tears. I rush to her, throwing the bear on the visitor chair, and I grab her in a hug as gently as I can. After a solid five minutes, we both pull back.

"I'm so, so sorry, Amber, I should have been faster. I should have been more aware of my surroundings. I wish I could take your place," I cry, wishing like hell I could make that happen.

"Fuck you! I'm the one who should be sorry. I didn't fight harder, and I let you get taken. You have nothing to be sorry for, I don't blame you. If it's anybody's fault, it's Stoney's. I would be happily on the streets of St. Louis, most likely getting arrested before I seal the deal, but I wouldn't be in this hospital bed."

I shake my head at her. "If it's *anybody's* fault, it's J's. You and I both know that Ryan wouldn't let anything happen to you if he could help it," I tell her gently. She sighs heavily and glares up at me. I don't let her glare dissuade me. She glances over at the chair and her brows furrow.

"Why did you bring me a bear that says 'It's a boy!'?" she asks me with a laugh, changing the subject. I cringe and give her a sheepish smile.

"Old habits, and all that," I say with a shrug, which she laughs hard at. She hisses due to the pain, and gives me a long look.

"What's wrong, sweets? You've got that sullen look about you. Tell Auntie Ambie all about it," Amber says confidently, like she's a therapist. I shake my head, not wanting to talk about it. She gestures to her bandaged chest. "Come on, bitch, I didn't get all Frankentitty, so you could keep shit from me. I did this for you. Talk to me."

"Frankentitty? You almost died, and you call yourself Frankentitty? Good lord, I was right, you *are* crazy." I stick out my tongue at her, but she just stares at me and waits. Finally, I sigh. "Collin told me he loved me just a little bit ago. After I found out he had someone searching for my father. My father was the thing of nightmares, and he went behind my back to find him. He wants to slay all my demons, and I just have nothing to offer him. I'm a homeless pickpocket. I'm nothing. I let my life go down the drain because I've been running from a ghost," I say dejectedly, finally giving voice to my fears and insecurities.

"And I'm a stripper-slash-wannabe prostitute. Life happens to the best of us, babes. You have strength and skill, but most of all, you have a man that loves you because of your crazy shit. He wants to fight your demons for you. Let him, sweets. If you don't like where you are in your life, change it. You're so young, sweets, you have time to change the world if you choose. Let him be by your side if he wants. Change your circumstances for yourself if that's what *you* want. But if he loves you now, can you imagine how much he's gonna love you when you get to where you're happy with yourself? Don't be afraid to love him back. He's not your father. He's a good man. Trust me," Amber tells me with raised brows.

I pause and let her words really sink in. I can become a better person for myself and still let him be in my life. He was trying to help me. God, I'm such a brat.

"How'd you get to be so smart, Amber Renee James?" I ask her with a smile.

"I watch a lot of porn and *The Bachelor*," she quips and I just laugh and shake my head. "I think you're my best friend, Zaydra. You want a fresh start, right? Live with me. Continue to see Collin if it makes you happy, or not. I want you to do what makes you happy. You're such a good person, and it helps that I get to see your tits all the time if you do. That way, I can tell my plastic surgeon what I'm really going for when I rectify my Frankentitties." She gives me a crazy smile.

"Okay, I'll live with you. Just don't cut my skin off in the middle of the night and wear it around. That's a dealbreaker to me," I say mockingly. Her smile grows wider, and if I didn't know her, it might be slightly creepy.

"I would do that in broad daylight, crazy woman. Light is

essential to not damage the skin when slicing." I roll my eyes at her Jeffrey Dahmer-esque statement. "So, now that that's decided, what song makes you horny, so I know what *not* to play when getting ready. It's important roommate information. Trust me, my last one used to play 'Sail' by AWOLNATION all the time, and I couldn't concentrate due to the slip n' slide in my panties. So out with it," Amber says, completely taking me by surprise, even though I know not to be. Finally, after thinking hard for a long minute, a song pops into my head.

"Probably 'Neon Moon,'" I tell her, and she blinks at me.

"The Brooks and Dunn song? You get off to the country broken heart song? What kind of monster are you, you weirdo?" she asks, cringing.

"No, it's by Cigarettes After Sex. Jesus, what kind of person do you think I am?" I tell her, laughing. She puts up one finger and grabs her cell phone. After a moment, the sounds of Brooks and Dunn crooning fills the room. She's laughing and wincing at the same time as I flip her off.

"What, this doesn't bring out the waterfall, sweets? Are you sure?" she says, gasping for breath between her laughing bouts. What a bitch. She's the one who asked me. I just glare at her until she cuts off the music, and I must look pretty fierce because her face sobers up. I realize she's looking behind me, and I turn to see Collin standing there, looking a little haggard, with stubble on his strong chin and tired eyes.

I look at Amber again and she makes the shooing motion. "Alrighty, you two, visiting hours are over. I can't have you here killing my flow while I try to mac on the good doctor. Hi, Doctor McSexyface!" she calls out to the doctor who just entered the room.

He stops in his tracks and waits for the nurse to catch up, like he doesn't trust Amber. His narrowed eyes are on her, until he moves his gaze to us.

"She's right, folks, it's past visiting hours, and you have to go. You can see Ms. James in the morning," Dr. Sexypants says.

Amber winks up at me, and mouths, "Told you he wants me."

I rise and leave the room, fully aware Collin is hot on my heels. I continue down the hallway to the elevator without saying a word. We both get on once the doors open and as soon as they close, Collin turns to me.

"I need you in my life, Zaydra. I won't fight your battles for you. I was just trying to make you less afraid to live your life." Collin starts to tell me more, but I hold my finger up to his lips. His eyes search mine.

"You love me?" I ask finally.

"More than I ever thought possible. I know that we've only known each other for a little while, but I can feel it in my soul. We were meant to meet, you were meant to help me find Cammie. I know fate brought us together. I know if you give me a chance, I'll love you with everything in me. I will do everything in my power to make you the happiest woman on this planet," Collin replies fiercely.

I nod after a minute or so. "That's good. It seems like I love you too," I respond and he blinks at me. "I'm sorry I overreacted earlier. I was madder at myself than you. I didn't think I deserved to have someone like you love me, but Amber and Miguel set me straight. I love you, Collin, to distraction. I'm going to better myself, for myself, but I also want to be somebody you're proud to love."

"You already are, baby. I'm so proud to love you, and that you love me. I'm the luckiest man alive, that it was my wallet you stole. I never expected you to steal my heart too," he replies with a wink as the elevator dings. I throw him a saucy smile over my shoulder as I exit.

"I've always been good at my job," I reply, and blow him a kiss.

FORTY-FOUR

COLLIN

THE ANXIETY OF ALMOST LOSING ZAYDRA TO MY OWN actions after I had just gotten her back keeps me up tonight. I stare down at her sleeping form in my arms, and I hold her tighter. My niece tuckered her out earlier, asking a million and one questions. She's decided she and Zaydra are best friends, and wants to be "a badass like Auntie Z" when she gets older. Collette is letting her get away with everything right now because having Cammie in front of her after so long, she would murder anybody who happened to bring down whatever was bringing Cammie sunshine. My sister can be vicious when she wants to be.

I'm relishing the feel of having the woman I love in my arms for what I'm hoping is the first of many nights to come. My thoughts are jolted as my phone starts buzzing. Seeing it's Mitchell has me hesitant to answer, after how the night went earlier when I did the first time. Not wanting to hide anymore, I answer with a quiet, "Reeves."

It wakes Zaydra up anyway. She glances up at me, startled from slumber. I mouth "Mitchell" at her and she sits up completely.

"Reeves, I found something else. This sicko had photographs

in his house. Multiple children, including his own, with him and those church buddies you told me about. This evidence here is pretty damning to all these men, but Collin, these pictures aren't that old. They might still have these girls. We're going to have to call the Feds. This is too big for me to handle alone," Mitchell tells me in a rush.

Usually, he's not the type of man to get any law enforcement involved, so I know these pictures have to be bad. I glance over at Zaydra, who appears to have heard every word. She straightens her shoulders and lifts her chin, nodding sharply at me.

"I'll call them. You don't have to be involved in that side, Mitchell." He exhales loudly and thanks me. "I appreciate your help here. Your payment will be in your account shortly," I tell him brusquely and end the call. I turn to face Zaydra fully, taking her small hand in mine. "If I make this call, you'll be involved. There are too many pictures of you for you not to be. There will be a trial, and you will have to relive it all again, but these bastards who hurt you will go to jail. Or I make it go away. Everything will burn to the ground, no one will hear from those men again, and no one has to know your story," I state, with a protectiveness inside me I didn't think was possible.

Zaydra is shaking her head at me adamantly. "I'm done running, Collin. What kind of role model would I be to Cammie if I run from this now? I was involved a long time ago. I'm ready to face these demons head-on. I'm not going to let these bastards win anymore. Let's see how they like prison. I want them to pay," she says fiercely.

I search her face, and kiss her quickly before I rise from the bed. I lumber over to the jeans I was wearing last night and pull out the card I was given. I hope everyone likes middle-of-the-night phone calls because soon, I doubt any of us will sleep much. Being confronted by the evil in humanity does that to you.

I dial the number and let my phone connect. When the

gruff voice laced with sleep answers, I say, "Rosenthal, I have a tip for you. I have evidence that there is another trafficking ring in the panhandle of Florida. Busting two in one week is going to get you and McCall a promotion. This one is on you, though. I'll give you the information. But this time, I can't be involved in the bust."

"Why is that?" Rosenthal asks gutturally.

With a grim smile at my woman, I reply calmly, "Because I would kill all the bastards and let God sort them out."

He grows silent for a moment, and my eyes drift back to Zaydra, who is coming towards me. She wraps her arms around me and kisses my chest. I close my eyes, loving the sensation. I dip down and capture her lips in a kiss, but Rosenthal's voice brings my mind back to the task at hand.

"If it's more personal this time, I can only guess it's because of your dark-headed lady love that got herself kidnapped last time. Don't worry, you won't be involved, but I'll keep you updated if you want. Just text me the address. I don't know if McCall and I will have jurisdiction, but we can try. Just one more thing, though. Take care of each other," he responds.

"Will do. Go fuck these guys' worlds up," I declare.

"With pleasure." Rosenthal ends the call. I throw my phone down on the table and turn to Zaydra. I pick her up and kiss her again, then toss her on the bed and she bounces. My eyes are momentarily distracted by her bouncing tits. Maybe the guys were right—it *is* about the tits.

Right now, though, she needs me to distract her from the bad in the world, the bad that's too close to home and honestly, I need a distraction from the thought of nobody saving her when she was Cammie's age. But she's fine and she's with me now, and I'm going to protect her from all the bad shit.

Happiness with her is like breathing; it's a subconscious thing. So, I do the only thing I'm capable of doing.

I take a deep breath.

SIX MONTHS LATER

ZAYDRA

I RUN AROUND IN A FLURRY OF ACTIVITY, IN THE apartment I share with Amber, while she lounges on the couch watching me lose my mind. I check under couch cushions and the random assortment of dildos that are on the loveseat. Yes, Amber keeps her dildos on the loveseat—she says that's what the name implies.

"Bitch, have you seen my other shoe?" I screech, trying to be heard over the loud-ass country music she has playing. She has taken to playing it anytime she wants to be funny. She finally mutes Luke Combs.

"No. Why don't you just wear mine? They'll look hot with that dress. Where are you going anyways?" Amber asks sweetly.

"I'm not wearing any more of your stripper heels. The last time I did, I almost fell and broke my face. And I don't know what Collin and I are doing; he said it's a surprise. I bet we're celebrating me getting my GED and applying to college," I tell her wistfully, pausing for a moment to daydream before I shake myself out of my musings and restart my search for the elusive unicorn shoe.

"I bet it's butt stuff. R-I-P your butthole," Amber tells me nonchalantly.

"*What?*"

"The surprise, I bet it's butt sex. R-I-P your butthole," Amber replies. I just stare at her for a moment, the one shoe I do have falling to the ground.

"I'm not doing butt stuff!" I yell.

She rears back with a smirk, and I whirl around to see what she's smiling at. Collin is standing there, laughing silently at me. My face grows hot. No matter how many times I see him, my heart skips a beat and my pussy clenches, making me want to jump him. Amber leans in to me, catching my eye again.

"Ohhhh. I get it. R-I-P *his* butthole! No judgment, sweets, whatever floats your freaky boat. Let that freak flag fly," Amber fake whispers to me while looking at Collin. My mouth drops open.

"Are you…are you kink shaming me?" Collin asks in disbelief, and I now know my best friend and my boyfriend have been hanging out entirely too much. Amber's musical laughter follows her out of the room.

"Are you about ready, baby?" Collin asks me. I give him a wince and he laughs, plopping down on the couch, more than willing to wait for my perpetually late ass. I hurry over and give him a quick kiss that has my heart beating faster.

"I just need to find my shoe. Thank you for being so great. I love you," I tell him in a rush, then resume my search. I finally see the elusive shoe, behind Amber's exercise ball she uses exactly never. I grab it and hold it up triumphantly. Collin claps at the delight on my face and I curtsy, then plop down next to him to put my shoes on.

"Have I told you how much I love you lately?" he asks suddenly. I give him a big grin and loop my arms around his neck, pulling myself on to his lap, and wiggle down to get comfortable. He groans and I laugh, then kiss him again.

"Just every day. Why, have you forgotten?" I sweetly respond, trying to be cute. Classy and sassy is my new daily mantra, so I might as well earn it.

He smiles at me in the way I love, his eyes crinkling at the corners, and says, "I would never forget. But I do have some news. The jury came back today. About an hour ago, actually. They convicted every single one of them. Rape in the first degree, human trafficking, assault in the first degree, kidnapping, aggravated sexual assault, and possession of child pornography. They're all going away for twenty-five years to life. You did it, baby. You did it."

I burst into tears, knowing this was a long time coming. I testified in front of the grand jury, then testified again at the trial a month ago, and I said I wouldn't go back. I feel vindicated. My life is completely my own again, without this dark cloud hanging over me.

"Wait, was that my surprise?" I ask him suddenly. He inclines his head to the side.

"Of course not. The surprise is later, when we do butt stuff," Collin says jokingly.

"*I knew it!*" we hear Amber shriek from the other room. Collin shakes his head and helps me to my feet. "Y'all have fun tonight. Collin, take care of my girl. At least until she comes to her senses and realizes she's a lesbian for me," Amber calls to us.

Collin mutters something about crazy girls, and I just laugh.

COLLIN

I'M SWEATING THROUGH MY SHIRT. I LEAD HER THROUGH the busy restaurant to the table I have reserved for us in the back. I don't normally get nervous but Zaydra's had a big month. She got her GED and applied for college to be a social worker, to work with young, trafficked girls. She has so much passion and direction, it's awe-inspiring to me. I fall for her more daily, and I'm afraid one day, she's going to realize she doesn't need me.

"Collin, this place is really nice. What's the occasion?" she asks me after we're seated.

I take a moment to appreciate the woman seated across from me, then I pull the folded file from my suit jacket pocket. I spread it out in front of her and show her the paperwork for my new venture. "Well, first off, it's our six-month anniversary today. So, for an anniversary gift, I decided to start a charity for youth trafficked victims," I tell her gently. "It's called Cammie's Promise. I listed you as the CEO, and I am going to be the silent partner funding it. When you're ready, once you graduate, you can take the reins and decide on this charity's future. This is yours; you deserve it."

"*What*?!" she screeches, forgetting where we are for a moment, and I chuckle at her outburst. "Collin…this is huge. I don't deserve this." She continues to scan the document in front of her, then she looks up at me, her eyes filling with tears threatening to fall. "This could really make a difference in so many lives. I can't believe you did this, for me. Why?"

"Because I love you." I slide a key across the table. "I want you to move in with me. I know you love living with Amber, I know it's fast, and you probably think I'm crazy, but I know I love you and I want to take this next step with you. I want to marry you, someday, because I know you aren't ready for that right now."

I reach over and take her hand in mine as a single tear falls down her cheek. "I want to go to bed at night, with you falling asleep in my arms, and I want to wake up because you've starfished on the bed and I've fallen off. I want to begin and end every single day the same way. With you. Please, say yes. You're over every day, anyway," I tease, squeezing her fingers.

She stares at me as slow tears streak down her face, and my body goes cold, afraid I've pushed too far too fast. Then she smiles. "I want that too. I can't believe how lucky I am, that I picked your pocket that night. Amber is too nice to tell me, but I know she wants her space back. She's a very private person."

I let out the breath I didn't know I had been holding and the muscles in my shoulders relax. "When you *do* ask me to marry you though, make sure we're in Vegas so we can do it immediately. I'm not good at waiting for things," she finishes, and I laugh heartily.

"Of course, baby, whatever you want. We can skip dinner and move you into my house right now, if you don't want to wait," I joke, and she smiles at me sheepishly.

"Are you sure you don't mind? I know exactly where I want everything, and I just need to do it right now," she asks with a shrug of her shoulders.

"Let's go then. That means we get to do butt stuff, though, right?" I say with a wink. She gets her deranged beauty queen look, and I know I should be afraid, but I just find her cute.

"Only if I get to sit on your face again," she whispers and I grin.

"Deal."

ACKNOWLEDGMENTS

This novel has been eight years in the making. I started writing it in college and finally finished it. When writers say that it takes a village, they aren't kidding. I had so much help along the way, and I really am incredibly blessed and grateful. There are so many people who had a hand in my typing "the end". Let's get to it then.

To BT Urruela and Theresa Hissong, thank you for holding the contest that led me to this moment. Thank you for picking this book and taking a chance on a snarky pickpocket and an ex military man. BT, thank you for deciding to have me and this book as the first novel under your publishing company, Epistula Publishing. It means the world to me.

To Golden Czermak, the one and only FuriousFotog, thank you for providing me with the beautiful cover of this book, and for helping my idea of Zaydra to come to life.

To Jenn Wood and All About the Edits, thank you for making sure this work of mine is polished and pretty!

Y'all rock!

To my sister, Amber; my one and only beta reader, thank you for believing in this book when I wasn't even sure it was going to be a book. Thank you for being my ride or die, and always telling me when something sucks, even when I was positive it was awesome. Thank you for trying to get my creative juices flowing by trying to introduce 'werewolves' into every situation. It still didn't work! Sorry for the whole no werewolves thing, maybe next time. Thank you.

To my family, thank you for feeding the creativity inside me when I was young. You all made it okay for me to be weird. Mom, thank you for letting me steal all of your romance novels, and when you caught me, thank you for just chuckling and handing me 'the better ones'. Looking at you Christine Feehan.

Kim, you really are the inspiration behind one of my characters, but I won't tell you which one! I love you all.

To Ryan, thank you for putting up with my writing reclusiveness, and encouraging me with every passing day. I'm still not writing you in. I love you though.

To Christy and Glenn, thank you for taking pride in my accomplishments, and cheering for me every step of the way. You are really the best friends I could ever ask for.

To Todd and Sabrina, thank you from the bottom of my heart for being so good to me. For giving me a second family, and for being so understanding of all of my life's ups and downs. Thank you for being in my corner when I announced that I was a writer, like a real one! Thank you for creating a work environment where creativity exists in spades and you don't have to look too hard for it. Some of my best ideas were born at work. I love you both.

To my work family, thank you all for being incredibly supportive when I told you I entered a contest. Thank you all for listening to me talk excitedly for hours when I won, even though you couldn't get away from it. Thank you for believing it was awesome when all of you knew nothing about it, just because you think I'm awesome. You all are the awesome ones.

Lastly, a humble thank you to any reader who purchases this book. This book is the product of sleepless nights, tears, and drunken write-a-thons. It's incredibly personal to me, and if you made the conscious decision to pay for this, I am forever grateful. No takebacks though! But in all seriousness, you all are who I write for, I hope you liked it! If you didn't, lie to me! I love each one of you. Hopefully you continue on this journey with me.

Xoxo,
Christa

ABOUT THE AUTHOR

Christa DeClue grew up in small town Missouri. She went to Truman State University to study Journalism. She freelanced for a few newspapers, before she settled in the panhandle of Florida. When she's not writing, she works with wine. Those are her two greatest loves. She's funny on paper but awkward in real life. This is her debut novel.

Made in the USA
Monee, IL
07 April 2021